SALLY DEFREITAS

The Deadliest Lake

Enjoy!

Sally DeFreitas

First published by Michigan Mysteries Press 2020

First edition

ISBN: 978-0-578-78519-6

This book was professionally typeset on Reedsy.
Find out more at reedsy.com

Prologue

H-O-M-E-S

That's how we were taught to remember the names of the five Great Lakes. The names are: Huron, Ontario, Michigan, Erie and Superior.

Left behind by glaciers at the end of the last ice age, each of the lakes holds a particular distinction: Erie is the shallowest, Superior is deepest, Huron has the longest shoreline, and Ontario is the smallest. But Lake Michigan has the dubious honor of being the deadliest for swimmers.

Sad, but true. As far as documented drownings that are not shipwreck related, Lake Michigan leads the pack every summer with twice as many swimming fatalities as the other four lakes combined. How can this be? Why is my favorite lake so deadly for swimmers?

There are a number of reasons for this unpleasant distinction.

First, consider that the lake has many miles of sandy beach that invite swimmers to take a dip, as opposed to, say, the rocky shores of Lake Superior. Second, consider the population density; both sides of the lake have major cities, with Chicago being the largest. Lake Michigan also has a wealth of smaller towns scattered along the shorelines of both Wisconsin and Michigan, which means there are many people living near the shores of this Great Lake who might venture out swimming.

Then there is the distinctive configuration. Lake Michigan has a long north/south axis, over three hundred miles long; and a short east/west axis, about a hundred miles across. Prevailing winds are from the west, so the wind blows from the Wisconsin side and pushes the water toward Michigan, where it builds up. This buildup eventually needs to return, creating a current that pulls away from shore. This current is commonly known as the riptide and can easily overpower the strongest of swimmers—dragging them out into the lake while they struggle to reach land.

CHAPTER ONE

The man from Chicago whistled a nameless tune as he sent a chewed up Frisbee flying down the beach and watched Murphy, his shepherd collie mix, jump with joy as she launched her furry body in pursuit of the disc, the two of them indulging in their favorite inter-species pastime. The dog never seemed to tire of the game, even when she had to retrieve the Frisbee from the water.

Looking up, the man saw that the rising sun had already cleared the dune to the east. The morning beach walk had always been one of his favorite rituals when he stayed at his Michigan cottage and, now that his wife was gone, it had become a form of solace. Like most summer visitors, he harbored fantasies of making a permanent home in Cedar County, and on this bright summer morning, he was entertaining that vision once again.

An excited bark from Murphy interrupted his daydream. She was standing over something she had found on the beach, whimpering, and then she let out a howl. He hurried closer to investigate, doubling his pace. Within a few seconds, he was able to see what his dog had discovered that had her so upset.

Since the man from Chicago had been a medic in the navy, he didn't have to touch the thing his dog was sniffing to know that it was a body; it appeared to be that of a fairly young male. It was also clear to him that there was nothing he nor anyone else could do for the young man. Except, of course, to notify the authorities.

CHAPTER TWO

I made a final revision to the piece I was writing, about a controversial village zoning ordinance, and then cast a wistful eye at the clock on the wall of the newsroom of the *Shagoni River News.* Not for the first time, I wondered how the ancient air conditioning unit could make so much noise and have so little effect. My armpits were damp, and my body odor had long ago overpowered whatever deodorant I was wearing.

Well, no matter, I was going to be out of here soon. It was close to quitting time and I had just finished the final story for our weekly paper, which would be out on the newsstands the following day. If my boss, Marge Enright, didn't show up soon, I might even head out a little early. Heaven knows I deserved it. I had certainly done my share of overtime.

Would anyone notice if I left?

Looking around, I decided that the office was pretty close to empty. Sylvia, who writes obituaries and handles the front desk, had already gone home—with permission, of course. Jake, our news editor, was covering a road commission meeting and had told us not to expect him back in today. Our advertising gal was off selling space in our special "Summer Fun" issue. Larry, the graphics guy, was in the back as far as I knew, but it was hard to tell because he never interacted with the rest of us anyhow.

So I shut down my computer, pushed back my chair, and looked around the windowless space we call the newsroom. Yep, all I had to do was lock the front door, turn on the answering machine, tell Larry to lock up the back and I could be on my way to my breezy porch swing and a tall glass of lemonade.

That's when the telephone rang.

I did my best to ignore the unpleasant sound. It was probably someone who wanted to place an ad—or lodge a complaint because their ad from last week had not drawn any responses, as though that must be our fault. I looked at the clock, which stood at ten minutes to five. Maybe if I didn't answer they would just give up and call back tomorrow.

But the ringing continued. That's when I heard Larry yell from his man-cave in the back. "Tracy—you there? How 'bout getting that phone?"

I was caught. So I picked up. "Tracy Quinn, Shagoni River News," I said sounding more civil than I felt. "How can I help you?"

The caller didn't identify himself, but the gruff voice left me no doubt that it was our news editor, Jake Billington. "Tracy, listen up, we've got a story here."

"Sure, Jake, but I was just leaving. Can it wait until tomorrow?"

"No, it can't wait. It needs to go in this issue."

"So it's breaking news?"

This was a standard joke between us since a weekly paper rarely catches anything that could qualify as breaking news. Except on election night.

But Jake was not in a joking mood. "Yes, it's breaking news," he said. "We've got an unidentified body."

****

Half an hour later, I put the finishing touch on the story that Jake had more or less dictated to me.

Tuesday morning a summer resident walking his dog on the beach near Sable Point discovered a body that appeared to have been washed ashore. The deceased was a young adult male dressed only in a pair of boxer shorts, and the body carried no identification. Cedar County sheriff Benny Dupree, who was at the scene, said his department had not yet received any reports about any missing persons.

Dupree said the man appeared to be in his early or mid-twenties, was about six feet tall and of average build. He also said the cause of death appeared to be drowning, although that cannot not be confirmed until an autopsy is completed. Dupree is asking anyone with information that might be helpful in this case to telephone the sheriff's department at (220) 3355-XXXX.

So now I was finished, except for a headline. I tried out *DEAD BODY WASHED*

UP ON BEACH...then switched to *BODY OF YOUNG MAN FOUND NEAR SABLE POINT*...and then *UNIDENTIFIED SWIMMER WASHES UP NEAR LIGHTHOUSE*. They were all a little too wordy, taking up too much space.

And besides, how young did someone have to be to qualify as *young*? And was *dead body* too repetitive, since the word body already pointed to it being dead? And had the body really washed up on the beach or had someone maybe dropped it there? Someone could have driven an ATV down the beach then dumped the body, and the tire marks would have washed out in an hour. Though that theory would definitely suggest something other than a tragic accident.

But now I was digressing and wasting my own time. It was not my job to solve this case, only to complete the story so I could go home. I settled for *BODY FOUND ON BEACH*, and then searched for a place to put the story.

Jake said it had to be on the front page, preferably near the top. That meant something had to be moved—so I shifted the meth lab bust to the bottom half of the page, and put the Crop Walk results on page two. This meant I had to eliminate one of the photos from that event. Hopefully, Larry would not be offended.

Jake had told me that Marge was coming in later, so I figured that if she didn't like what I had done, she would change it. Our editor never worried about hurting my feelings. With that thought I saved the new page I had created, locked up and got out of the office an hour later than I had planned.

Because my little Honda Civic had been sitting in the sun, the temperature inside was probably somewhere over a hundred degrees, so I rolled down the windows. The trip was over in a few minutes, and I heaved a sigh of relief as I parked in the shade of a spreading maple tree—a tree my grandfather had planted many years ago, shortly after the birth of my mother, his only child.

My house, a rambling two-story affair, sat on a little rise facing west that boasted an expansive lawn with half a dozen maples, a pair of majestic oaks, and a border of lilac bushes. At times I felt resentful because of all the care the place required, but most of the time I was just happy, for the first time in my life, to own a house.

I climbed the front steps and eased into the porch swing, which emitted a familiar squeak as it took my weight. The house had just enough elevation to catch the breeze that was almost always coming off Lake Michigan, the tourist magnet that filled our town with visitors every summer.

"Is that you, Tracy?"

Since I live alone, the sound startled me, but only for a moment. The voice had come from the kitchen window, which was open.

"Yes, it's me," I replied. "And what are you up to?"

"I'm making lasagna for supper."

My ex-stepdaughter Brooke had taken temporary refuge with me a few years before and had decided that the village of Shagoni River, with its buffet of seasonal jobs, was the ideal place for a college student to spend summer vacations. She had done so ever since. As a loner, it always took me a while to adjust to having another person in my territory and, just about the time that I did, she would go back to school and the house would feel empty.

I went inside and made my way back to the kitchen. I found Brooke there, looking beautiful as only the young can look, dressed in cut-offs and a tank top, her auburn hair curled into ringlets by the steam rising up from the pot she was stirring.

"I thought you were working second shift today," I said.

"Things got changed." She looked up, smiled, and blew a strand of hair away from her forehead. "I went in this morning and did the day shift."

"Was that before I got up? I didn't even hear you."

"I tried to be quiet."

"Thanks for that. So, how do you like working at the park?"

Our little town boasted a state park with an extensive campground that bordered a stretch of Lake Michigan with a white sand beach. Brooke had applied there for three seasons before she finally made the grade. "I like it," she said. " And it certainly pays better than all the ice-cream stores and coffee shops where I worked before." She moved away from the stove and poured the steaming sauce over pasta in a baking dish. "Sometimes things get a little hairy with us trying to enforce the quiet hours, and sometimes—well, you wouldn't believe the trash people leave on the beach."

"I'm glad you like it—since you waited so long to get in." I opened the refrigerator and found a can of soda, opened it and took a long swallow. "I'm surprised you felt like cooking on such a hot day."

Brooke slid the baking dish into the oven and straightened up before she answered. "Well, I sort of invited Derek over for supper." Then she added, "I hope that's okay with you."

"Of course it's okay. You know I like Derek."

Derek was the son of my best friend, Jewell, and ever since Brooke had made her appearance in town four years ago, the two of them had managed to spend a large part of their free time together every summer. "Okay, then, no problem." Brooke pulled a pitcher of lemonade from the refrigerator and poured herself a glass. "I've already put together a salad."

"Well, that's good. I'm ready to get out of the kitchen."

"It is toasty in here, isn't it?"

"Rather like an oven, I'd say."

She laughed that throaty laugh of hers. We took our drinks and decamped to the picnic table in the backyard, exiting through the screen door. "This should work," she said as she sat down. "I'm close enough that I should be able to smell if anything starts burning."

"I think we did have a small fire once, didn't we?"

"I guess we did—but that was because of that dumb cop out front telling you to cut down your milkweed. I got a little distracted."

"After your lecture about monarch butterflies, the cops never bothered me again."

"So there."

"All showing the advantage of a college education. Hey, I'm sorry I didn't make it to your graduation." Brooke had recently completed her four-year degree at a liberal arts college in Arizona.

"Oh, Tracy, you don't need to feel bad about that. Derek came up from Phoenix, and my mom was there, and she brought a couple of my aunts and a cousin I barely remembered. Then my dad showed up too, so it was just a tiny bit awkward dealing with both my parents at once."

"Guess you didn't need your dad's second ex-wife on the scene to complicate matters."

"Honestly, Tracy, you have always been my favorite stepmother."

"Thanks, sweetie. I'll use you for a reference next time I apply for a job."

Brooke got up and went inside, returning a few minutes later. "Good thing I checked," she said. "I moved the dish to a lower shelf."

"It looks like an awful lot of food."

"I just followed the recipe I found in your grandma's cookbook. But also, I was thinking we should invite Frank for supper. He always seems to appreciate a home cooked meal."

"Oh, um, Frank?"

"Yes, Frank, your boyfriend. So give him a call."

Suddenly I was staring at my soda can, reading the fine print. "Not tonight."

"Why not? Is he out of town?"

"I don't think so. But then again, he might be—out of town, that is." All the time I was thinking that I sounded like a tongue-tied idiot.

"Hey, what's going on? I thought you two were engaged."

I took a deep breath, playing for time while I searched for words. Finally I said, "Brooke, what's going on right now is—well, it seems like—it seems that Frank and I are not—we're not exactly speaking to each other right now."

CHAPTER THREE

After hearing the jumbled report about the status of my love life, Brooke regarded me in silence for a few minutes. Then she shrugged and said, "I guess that explains why you're not wearing that big honking ring he gave you."

I stared at my bare left hand. "Oh that—well, that wasn't actually—it wasn't technically an engagement ring."

"Sure looked like it to me. And I must say, this is disappointing. Here I've been waiting all this time to be your flower girl or your bridesmaid—or whatever honorary position you want me to fill."

"I guess maybe—" I felt my eyes burning and choked up a bit, then started over again. "Actually I don't know what to say."

"Do you want to talk about it?"

I shook my head. The idea of sharing my romantic troubles with this girl barely out of her teens made me feel ridiculous. "Um, thanks, but it's not—it's not something I can talk about right now." I finished my drink and stood. "I'm going to shower and stretch out for a few minutes. Call me when supper's ready."

"Okay, fine. I'll do that."

I left Brooke and headed for my bedroom, hoping she had not taken offense at my dismissal of her offer of counseling. Probably not. Young people are usually pretty resilient. My houseguest had brought up a subject I was trying my best to ignore. My thoughts were scattered as I stripped off my clothes and stepped into the shower.

That's when I heard a vehicle in the driveway, emitting explosive sounds as the engine was cut. Seconds later there were footsteps on the porch and a knock on the door.

"Anybody home?"

"Is that you, Derek?" Brooke called out. "Come on in."

I heard laughing and whooping as the two greeted each other. Once out of the shower, I dried off and put on shorts and a tee shirt. When I got to the kitchen I found Derek pulling plates out of the cupboard to set the table.

"Hey, Tracy," he said, his face lighting up with his distinctive, goofy grin.

"Hey yourself." He put down the plates and wrapped me in a bear hug which reminded me that Derek was no longer the gangly teenager I had met a few years ago. His shoulders were broader, and his upper lip showed a hint of moustache.

"You're looking good," I said. "That Arizona sun must agree with you."

"Phoenix is great in the winter," he said. "But right now, in July, it's pure hell. I'm happy to be here, spending a lot of time in Lake Michigan. Also, being around Brooke."

She gave him a playful punch and handed him a pair of oven mitts. "Okay," she said, "it's time for you to earn your dinner." With Brooke holding the oven door open, Derek reached in, pulled out the steaming casserole and placed it on the table.

"So, how do you like your job?" I said to Derek. "You know, you nearly broke your father's heart when you dropped out of college."

"I know—but he's getting over it."

"That's good. How do you like being an EMT?"

"I like it, mostly. And I'm taking classes to upgrade to paramedic."

"Your mom said you're working the night shift."

"I am. Working nights is fun, and I avoid the worst of the heat."

"How much time off do you have?"

"Only two weeks. But I managed the stretch that into seventeen days."

"Not near enough," said Brooke.

"Yes, and that's how it is in the real world. I don't have the whole summer off like Miss College Student over here." Derek took a make-believe swat at her with one of the mitts.

"Hey," said Brooke, "I'm working too."

"Oh, sure. Hanging at the beach every day. Flirting with the life guards."

"We don't have life guards, silly, and my job is more like emptying stinky trash cans. Plus, I'm hardly a guy magnet in that ugly uniform I have to wear."

"Speaking of flirting," she said, "did you get to that beach party Saturday night?"

"The one I invited you to but you were too busy to attend?"

"Well, yeah, I was working the late shift."

"Too bad. Yes, the party was great—once I found it—which took me about an hour."

"So where was it?"

"At somebody's cottage on Lake Michigan. Somewhere south of here but—you know—on a dirt road that didn't have a name, at a cottage that didn't have a number."

"Sounds like a secret location."

"Not much of a secret—there were tons of people there."

"Anyone I might know?"

"I doubt it. People were coming and going all night, but hardly anyone that I recognized."

"So how was it?"

"Just the usual—hot dogs, beer, bonfire at the beach..."

"Oh sure. You're just trying to make me feel better." Brooke surveyed the table. "Anyway, we're almost ready to eat. Would you get the water from the fridge and fill our glasses?"

That's when I noticed something that had so far escaped my attention. The table was set for four—definitely one more than the current population of my kitchen. I felt a flash of anger as I wondered if Brooke had been so bold as to call Frank on her own.

Making a major effort to keep my tone neutral, I said, "Hey, who's the extra place for?"

"Oh, that was my idea," said Derek. "I invited a friend."

"I see. Anyone I might know?"

"Probably not. His name is Scott."

"Scott who?" I said, relieved that no one had invited Frank. *Or was I disappointed?*

"I can't even remember his last name," said Derek. "I just ran into him at the beach today."

"And we have plenty of food," said Brooke.

"I hope you don't mind," Derek said to me.

"No, I don't mind," I said.

That seemed to settle the matter, so I selected a few bottles of salad dressing while Brooke tossed the salad and Derek filled our water glasses.

"I told Scott we wouldn't wait for him," said Derek. "He'd just got to the beach, and you know how easy it is to lose track of time down there."

"Especially this time of year," said Brooke, "when the daylight seems to go on forever."

"How well do you know this guy?" I said.

"Not very well," said Derek. "Remember how I did a year at Michigan State?"

"I remember. I met you about the time you dropped out."

"So I guess Scott and I had a class together...probably English Comp. And then he recognized me today and we got to talking while we were in line for ice cream. Here, let me do that." Derek picked up a large spoon and dug into the casserole.

The lasagna was so hot it sent up a cloud of steam when it hit my plate. "Better let that cool a minute," said Brooke.

"Don't worry, I will," I said as I turned my attention to the salad. That's when the telephone rang.

"Do you think that's him?" she said.

"Nope," said Derek, shaking his head. "He wouldn't know this number."

"It's probably Marge," I said. "My editor has a way of knowing when I sit down to eat."

"Look at it this way," said Derek as I pushed back my chair. "It'll give your food a chance to cool."

"Yeah, right," I grumbled on my way to the living room. I picked up the phone, fully expecting to hear my editor barking out a question or a criticism or, worst of all, an order to come back into the office.

But it wasn't Marge on the other end of the line. It was Frank, my estranged boyfriend, or whatever the hell he was at the moment.

****

"Tracy, how are you?"

My knees felt suddenly weak when I heard Frank's gravelly voice on the other end of the line. I eased myself into the recliner and took a deep breath before I answered. "I'm okay, Frank, except for—well, you know what—"

"Yeah, me too. I think—"

But I missed the rest of his sentence because my attention was diverted by the sound of somebody pounding on the front door. I put my hand over the receiver and yelled in the general direction of the kitchen, "Hey, somebody get the door."

My voice must have carried, because the next thing I heard was a chair scraping away from the table, followed by footsteps in the hallway. I turned my attention back to the telephone. "Frank, are you still there?"

"Yep, still here."

Derek reached the front door, and when he opened it, I saw him greeting a stocky blonde guy with a shaggy haircut.

"Frank," I said, "we really do need to talk—but this is not a good time for me. Things are kind of busy here right now."

"What's going on at your house?"

What does he think? That I have guys lined up begging me for dates? "I guess you know that Brooke's here."

"Sure, I saw her last week."

"Right. So Brooke made dinner tonight and invited Derek over. And then he invited someone else. Someone I don't know."

"Okay," said Frank. "Sounds like you have your hands full. I'm down in Lansing right now anyway. Are you free tomorrow—tomorrow evening, I mean?"

"I think so. I mean yes, as far as I know." *Was I trying not to sound too eager?*

"So how about dinner?"

"Dinner tomorrow—umm. I mean, dinner sounds great."

"Okay. I'll pick you up about six thirty."

"Great. I'll be ready." Suddenly I felt as though a weight had been lifted from my chest.

"And we'll talk."

"Yes, Frank, we need to talk."

"All right. Guess I'd better let you go now."

"Hey, I'm really glad you called."

"Me too. Say hello to Derek for me."

I returned to the kitchen feeling immensely better but also wondering what to say if Brooke started to quiz me about the phone call. Though I needn't have worried, because I found that both she and Derek were busy talking to our dinner guest.

Derek introduced me to his new friend. The guy was probably in his twenties, but those puppy-dog eyes and chubby cheeks made me think of him as somebody's baby brother.

"Tracy," said Derek, "this is my friend Scott Walker. And Scott, this is Tracy Quinn, who happens to own this house."

Scott, who was a little shorter than me, gazed at me with limpid brown eyes and smiled as he shook my hand. "I'm so pleased to meet you. This is a beautiful house you have here."

It seemed as though Scott held my hand a nanosecond longer than was strictly necessary, but perhaps it was I who didn't let go quite on schedule. "Thanks," I said. "It's nice to hear that from somebody. When you live in a place, you begin to lose sight of its beauty."

"It's always been a dream of mine," he said, "to someday have a house like this."

"Let me warn you," I replied, "old houses are sort of like old people—always developing problems and having things break down."

"Let's go ahead and eat," Brooke said, directing Scott to the empty seat.

"Sure thing," he said. But before he sat down, Scott pulled out my chair and held it for me, deftly sliding it into place as I sat down. I had to admit I was a little impressed with his manners.

By this time the lasagna on my plate had reached the perfect temperature. The salad was crispy, and the bakery rolls fresh and soft. Throughout the meal, the three of us pretty much took turns lobbing questions at our visitor, who seemed happy to fill us in. Scott told us that he had a sister a few years younger than him, had grown up in a small town near Big Rapids, and had just finished his degree at Michigan State. "My degree is in business," he said, "with an emphasis on the business of sports."

"And what does that qualify you for?"

"Good question," he said. "Mainly, I like golf, and I was hoping to get a job at a golf course this summer—you know, giving lessons and managing the pro shop. But by the time I got my applications out, it seems that all the spots were filled."

"So how did you end up over here?" said Brooke.

"Pretty much by accident," he replied with a grin. "My fallback plan was to visit my cousin in California before I settled down to look for a job. But then my car broke down, and by the time I got it running again, I didn't have enough money for a trip—or anything else, for that matter. For a while I thought I might have to move back in with my parents."

"A fate worse than death," said Derek.

"Sounds like you've met my parents," said Scott, and we all laughed. Our dinner guest was doing a good job of entertaining us.

"So what happened?" said Brooke.

"I got lucky. My uncle called me because he had just bought a produce stand over here. It's sort of a retirement venture for him and my aunt."

"That one just north of town?"

"That's the one. So they hired me as manager for the summer."

"Manager," said Brooke. "That's an impressive title."

"I think they just wanted someone for the heavy lifting."

"But anyway, here you are," she said.

"Right. I get a place to live and all the watermelon I can eat."

"Sounds like a good deal," said Derek.

"It's working out so far," Scott said as he reached for a second helping of lasagna. "This food is delicious, Brooke, thanks for cooking—and Derek, thanks for inviting me. I feel lucky that I ran into you on the beach today."

"Sure," said Derek. "But come to think of it, I might have seen you around here before this afternoon."

"It's possible. I came out in the middle of June."

"I keep thinking that I saw you Saturday night."

"I don't think so," said Scott. "Where were you?"

"At a beach party—down by the light house."

"Oh, that one. I heard about it. Really wanted to go and then I couldn't make it."

"Too bad. We had a good time."

"I'm sure it was more fun than my cousin's birthday party...but I pretty much had to be there. That's the downside of working for family."

"Who wants carrot cake?" said Brooke.

I declined dessert, so the three of them enjoyed the cake while I had a cup of tea.

"What a great meal," said Scott. "I really lucked out with you guys."

"Yes, you did," said Derek, "and don't you forget it."

"Hey," said Scott, "I saw a flyer for a free concert tonight in Ludington."

"What kind of music?" said Derek.

"I'm not sure. The band is called Stolen Horses, so I guess it might be some kind of country rock."

"Not exactly my thing," said Derek.

"Well, I'd like to hear them," said Brooke. "I think I deserve a night out."

"I'm sure you do," said Scott. "Tell you what—I'll take you to Ludington, and Derek can come along if he wants to."

"Oh, don't think you can go without me," said Derek.

"Want to come with us?" Brooke said to me.

"Thanks, but no thanks. I'm ready to put my feet up and read a book tonight."

I headed out to the backyard and watered my mini-garden while the three of them made a lot of raucous noise as they cleaned up in the kitchen.

Then Brooke called out, "Okay, Tracy, we're going. Sure you don't want to come with us?"

“I’m sure,” I said. “You guys have fun.”

CHAPTER FOUR

The next day at work I found myself humming a happy tune.

Anticipating my dinner date with Frank put me into a good mood—so good that I had to remind myself that I was still angry with him. Maybe we would go to the Captain's Table, our town's most upscale restaurant. I decided on what to wear and then changed my mind several times throughout the day.

Finally I was home. I skipped up the steps and across the porch, giving the swing a lighthearted shove as I passed by.

I tore through the house and into the bathroom, where I hopped in the shower, shampooed my hair, then toweled it dry and sprayed it with mousse with plans to arrange it into a style that would be gorgeous—well, if not gorgeous, at least sexy or maybe sophisticated or at least possibly cute. I even spread something on my face called avocado masque—a green goo that was guaranteed to make me look ten years younger.

While that product was drying and I was still wrapped in a towel, I meandered into the living room, where I noticed something I had overlooked on my mad dash to the bathroom—the message light on the phone was blinking.

Well, of course—that would be Frank, calling to confirm the time or telling me that he might be late or maybe asking me where I wanted to go for dinner. I pushed the button. It was Frank's voice that I heard. But his words were a crushing blow to my happy expectations.

"Tracy," he said, "I'm really sorry, but I'm not going to make it tonight. The sheriff said we have a meeting at six and I should clear my calendar for the evening because it might take some time. Believe me, I am sorry."

"Damn you, Sheriff Benny," I said, directing my words at the silver box on my telephone table. It wasn't the first time that Benny Dupree had interfered in my love life. As a reporter I needed to maintain a working relationship with the sheriff of Cedar County—and I did. But with Frank being his detective and me being the detective's girlfriend, there were times like this when I felt that the sheriff had outranked me and outflanked me.

So now I was close to tears, furious with Benny as well as mad at Frank. Also, cruelly disappointed that all of my beauty preparations were for naught—but also oddly grateful that Brooke wasn't around to see me in my churlish state. I headed to the bathroom to wash off the green mud, which appeared to have done nothing for my complexion other than giving me a shiny red nose.

That's when the telephone rang. I stared at it for a moment—simultaneously filled with hope but unwilling to risk another disappointment. When I finally picked up, I was greeted by the always comforting voice of my best friend Jewell. "Tracy, how are you?"

"To be honest, I am in a totally crappy mood." I never had to mince words with Jewell.

"Oh, is this a bad time?"

"Jewell, it's actually a good time. There's no one in the world I would rather talk to."

"So, tell me what's going on. I hope you're not getting tired of having Derek around so much."

"Oh no. Nothing to do with the kids. It's—well—it's about Frank."

"Ah, a lover's quarrel. Tell me all about it."

"I hardly know where to start. Except that we had a spat last week and have been ignoring each other ever since. Then yesterday he called and asked me out to dinner."

"Sounds promising. Did he apologize?"

"Not exactly. But he agreed that we need to talk."

"That sounds like a step in the right direction."

"Oh sure. But now he just called and cancelled."

"Oh no. Poor form on his part." Jewell's voice took on a soothing tone.

"Very poor form. Did he give a reason?"

"It was a meeting with Sheriff Benny. But the whole thing was just a message on my machine."

"Oh—and this leaves you no chance to vent."

"Right. So now I'm just sitting here steaming."

"Hey, forget about Frank. How about you and I go somewhere for dinner?"

"Really? Tonight?"

"That's why I called. I'm just leaving work, and Paul said he won't be home until late. Are you free?"

"Of course I'm free."

"Great. I'll pick you up in half an hour."

By the time Jewell arrived, I had the last of the green goo off my face, and with it had gone a lot of my bad mood. We sat on my porch and drank iced tea while she told me about the latest crisis in her job as director of nursing at Cedar County Hospital.

"But enough about me," she said. "What on earth is happening with you and Frank? The last time we were all together, I got the feeling that you and Frank were getting ready to move things forward."

"I guess we were talking pretty serious at the time."

"So what happened?"

"It has to do with—oh, I don't know if I'm being silly or not—but it has to do with Frank and his ex-wife."

"I guess that could be a real monkey wrench."

"Look," I said, "this is hard for me to talk about. I think I need a drink first."

"Sure. Let's go to La Senorita. They make a mean margarita."

"Sounds like just what I need."

Half an hour later, Jewell and I were seated in our favorite booth at our favorite restaurant and I was well into one of my favorite drinks.

"Here's what happened," I said. "Frank's daughter Sandra called him, because her son Peter was in trouble."

"That would be Frank's grandson. What kind of trouble?"

"Some kind of vandalism, I guess. But it was serious enough to have the police involved."

"How old is the boy?"

"Almost twelve. So one day last week, Thursday, I think, Frank went down to Grand Rapids after work to meet with Sandra—and then the ex-wife Jillian showed up too. After they all talked, it was pretty late and it seemed that Peter was due in juvenile court the next morning so, long story short, Frank decided to stay over—and he spent the night at Jillian's house."

We went silent for a moment while the waiter delivered our food...fish tacos for Jewell and a cheesy enchilada for me.

We started to eat and Jewell returned to the subject at hand. "Okay," she said, "is this what has you in a tizzy? The sleepover?"

"Well, yes, of course. Isn't it obvious that the arrangement would offer them a great opportunity for some hanky-panky?"

Jewell's next comment cut to the heart of the matter. "You mean you don't trust Frank?"

"Oh, Jewell, I honestly thought that I did. But then this thing—it just kind of hit me the wrong way."

"Okay, but first tell me one thing. How did you learn about this...overnight at Jillian's house?"

"Frank told me about it. He was back in town the next day, and we went out for supper and he told me about Peter and the whole business."

Jewell laid down her fork and looked at me across the table. "Do you want to hear my take on this?"

"Of course. That's why I'm spilling my guts. I haven't told anyone else, not even Brooke."

"Here's what I think—I'm pretty sure you have nothing to worry about."

"What makes you say that?"

"Tracy, here's the thing. If Frank had anything to hide, he never would have told you where he spent the night. He could have said that he stayed with his daughter or that he went to a motel—but, in fact, his conscience was clear, so he told you the truth."

I thought about her words while I signaled for another drink. "It's a good theory," I said, "and I guess it does make sense. But now, if you're right, I feel really stupid for wasting so much energy being mad at him for a whole week."

"There's no need to berate yourself. Love can make a fool of anybody."

I was feeling better as we shared a piece of chocolate cake and then Jewell drove us to the state park. I carried my sandals while we walked on the beach, and afterward we sat on a bench to enjoy the sunset. The sky turned cloudy but showed some interesting shades of orange and purple before we left. By the time we arrived back on my street, the daylight was almost gone.

"Aha," said Jewell, "it looks like you have company."

"I think you may be right," I said when I made out a bulky figure sitting on the steps of my front porch.

She pulled to a stop. "Do you want me to come with you?"

"Thanks for the offer, but I think I'm ready to handle this—thanks to our anger management session."

"Remember, Tracy, he's just a man."

"I'll remember," I said as I got out of her car. "And thanks again. Thanks for everything."

"Let me know how this turns out," she said just before she drove away.

I took a deep breath and walked up the hill to confront my estranged boyfriend, Frank Kolowsky.

******

Frank stood as I approached and said, "Hey, good to see you."

Just out of habit I walked into his arms. Frank is taller than me, which I appreciate, because all through high school I towered over my classmates and I now stand five feet ten in my Birkenstocks. Frank also has enough bulk to provide a comforting hug.

"Good to see you, too," I said. "Long meeting with Benny?"

"Yep. It was about a body that washed up on the beach down south of here."

"I know. I helped write it up for the paper. Do they know who it was?"

"Not yet. We'll be looking at missing person reports."

"Did you have any supper?"

"Nope. Just a donut and coffee."

"Poor baby. You must be starved."

"I am," he said, patting his ample mid-section.

"Come on inside. Should be some leftover lasagna."

"Sounds wonderful," he said as we entered the house. "But are you still mad at me?"

"I am. But I won't attack while you have an empty stomach."

Frank followed me into the kitchen, and we put the microwave to work, heating up lasagna and leftover pizza and some scalloped potatoes. I sat down and had a cup of coffee while he consumed everything I put in front of him. I like a man who has an unfussy appetite.

"I talked to Jewell," I said, "and she convinced me that you probably did not sleep with your ex-wife. But it just bothered me that you stayed at her house."

"Yeah. I definitely got that part. And you were pretty emotional about the whole thing."

"Well, it just struck me the wrong way."

"I guess I didn't explain it very well, but may I remind you that your ex-husband stayed with you one night last winter."

"Um, it was the winter before."

"Okay, but wasn't that the same thing?"

"I guess you could say that. But it wasn't anything we planned. It was just a cold night and it got late and, well, it was circumstances."

"Exactly," he said. "It was the same for me last week."

"Maybe it was. But I made Steven sleep upstairs in a cold bedroom."

"Well, ours was about the same. She made me sleep in the den on something called a futon. My back hasn't been the same since." Frank demonstrated his discomfort with a bent neck, twisted shoulder and a pained look on his face.

His distortions made me laugh—and it felt good to let go of my anger. "Okay," I said. "It sounds like we are about even. So, what's happening with your grandson? Did anything get settled?"

"Looks like he'll be on probation for a while and have to do some community service."

I found a bottle of wine and poured two glasses, which we took into the living room, where we settled on the couch. Just as we were moving into a clinch, we were interrupted by the sound of a vehicle, followed by laughter and high-spirited voices.

"I expect that will be Brooke and Derek," I said as I made an attempt to rearrange myself.

As it turned out, I was only half right. Seconds later, Brooke arrived with a young man in tow. This time her companion was not Derek, but her new friend Scott. They bumped the screen door open as they came inside because they both had their arms filled with large paper bags.

"Oh, Frank," she said when she spotted us. "You're here. That's great—I mean—I hope we're not interrupting anything."

"It wouldn't be the first time," he said.

She giggled. "Anyway, Frank, this is my friend Scott. Scott this is Frank, Frank Kolowsky." Scott set down his bag and the two men shook hands. "And look what he's giving us," Brooke said as she pulled two quart boxes out of her sack. "We've got cherries and berries."

"And apricots and peaches," said Scott as he reached into his bag. "Just try these." He brought out a handful of apricots and handed samples to me and Frank. I bit into an apricot and soon had juice running down my chin.

"I'm going to try to make a peach pie," said Brooke.

"I'm sure it will be great," said Frank. "I still remember your peach cobbler."

"How was the concert last night?" I said.

"I really liked it—and Scott did too. Derek, well, not so much, but that's his problem, I guess." She and Scott shared a giggle. "Tonight we just went out to the river and then stopped so I could meet Scott's aunt and uncle. And look what they gave us. I had to turn down the watermelon because we couldn't carry any more. Is it okay if I make room in the bottom of the fridge for the berries?"

My mouth was full, so I nodded my answer.

"I hope you guys didn't steal this stuff," said Frank as he started on his third apricot.

"Don't mind him," I said as I dabbed my chin with a tissue. "He's a cop."

"Are you really a cop?" said Scott.

"Yes. I'm with the Cedar County Sheriff's Department."

"Well, I didn't steal anything," he said. "This stuff is all surplus, so I'm doing everyone a favor." He explained about his job at his uncle's fruit stand, and the two of them engaged in a few minutes of conversation about peach pie, the hot weather, and the possibility of rain. Then Brooke and Scott took their bags to the kitchen. There was the sound of the refrigerator door opening and closing, and then it sounded like they were making popcorn.

"He seems like a nice young man," said Frank.

"Oh, you're just impressed by his fruit connection. I can tell you are drooling at the prospect of peach pie."

"Nothing wrong with that," he said just before he kissed me.

"Nothing wrong with that either," I said when I had recovered my breath.

CHAPTER FIVE

"Hotter than hell today," grumbled Benny Dupree as he guided the Cedar County Sheriff's car off the freeway and onto the Grand Rapids exit.

His passenger, Frank Kolowsky, tended to agree. "Are you sure the AC is turned on?" he said as he fiddled with the dials on the dash.

"Oh, it's turned on all right," said the sheriff, "but the damn thing is nearly useless in this weather."

"We should have made this trip first thing in the morning."

"That's what I wanted to do, but the young lady in question said she couldn't possibly meet us before three o'clock."

"Which is pretty much the hottest time of the day."

"Yeah, and now she'll probably be late. Women always are."

Frank thought that Benny had not absorbed much from the gender sensitivity training the entire department had been subjected to. But he didn't say so. What he said was, "Well, at least it'll be cold inside."

"Oh yeah, we'll be shivering soon. I just hope she doesn't get all blubbery."

"If she does, it's your job to console her. Did you bring some tissues?"

"Like hell. That's why I brought you along. Anyway, I told her to bring a friend. Wait a minute—did I miss my turn back there?"

"Nope, we're good. Go two more blocks and then left at the stoplight."

"I hate driving in this town."

"We're okay. It's a straight shot from here."

Minutes later Benny pulled into a nearly empty parking lot bordered by scraggly trees on one side and a windowless building on the other. Smack dab in the center of the lot was a small yellow car. "Reckon that's it?" said Benny as he parked the cruiser.

"Yep. Said she drove a Kia."

"Damn silly car."

"At least she's on time," said Frank. "What's her name?"

"Her name is—ah something funny, like a pole dancer. Candy or Brandi." Benny consulted his notes. "Brandi Fairchild."

"Okay," said Frank as he climbed out. "Let's go meet Brandi."

Two young women had exited the yellow car and stood waiting as Frank and Benny approached. One of them was short and plump with curly red hair, the other one tall and willowy. Both wore tank tops and jeans with holes in the knees.

"Good afternoon, ladies," Frank said as he approached. "We're with the Cedar County Sheriff's Department, and we're looking for Brandi Fairchild."

"That'll be me," said the redhead. She stepped forward but did not acknowledge his outstretched hand.

"Okay," said Frank, "and thanks for meeting us here. I guess you know this is going to be difficult no matter how it turns out." He nodded toward the building. "Let's step inside. There's a room...sort of a waiting room, where we can talk before we—well, first we need to ask you some questions."

The four of them walked to the featureless building and stopped at the door, which boasted a sign that said *AUTHORIZED PERSONNEL ONLY*. Benny pushed a button, spoke to an intercom and, seconds later, was rewarded with a loud buzz. Frank pulled the door open and held it while they all walked inside. The room they entered had cement block walls and, in one corner, a collection of orange plastic chairs.

They ignored the chairs and stood while the sheriff asked questions and Frank made notes in his tiny spiral notebook. Brandi's friend gave her name as Leah Franklin. They showed their driver's licenses and said they were both students at Ferris State College.

Benny coughed and said, "Guess you know why we're here. Tuesday we found a body on the shore of Lake Michigan. We're trying to identify it. It's a young man, about six feet tall. Does that sound like it could be your—friend?"

Brandi nodded silently and bit her lower lip.

"And what is your boyfriend's name?"

Brandi sniffed and blew her nose. "His name is Tony—Tony Braxton."

"And when did you last see your boyfriend?"

"He's not my boyfriend," she said, her voice rising in volume. "He's my fiancé. We're planning to get married this Christmas."

"Sure," said Frank, "your fiancé. And when was the last time you saw him—Tony?"

"It was Friday. We had supper at my place, and then he went out with the guys. We both sort of do our own thing on Friday nights, but he always comes home—even if it's late. But this time he didn't. So Saturday afternoon I finally called Kevin—that's the friend he sometimes crashes with. Kevin hadn't seen him since Friday night either."

"Did you talk to these guys—the ones he went out with?"

She nodded. "I talked with his buddy Jeremiah. He said they had a few beers at the Pit Stop and Tony left about one a.m. They thought he was going to my place." She started crying and couldn't seem to stop, so her friend Leah took over the story.

"Tony's parents are out of town, but on Sunday we drove out to their house to see if he was there. He wasn't. So on Monday we finally went to the police."

"Is there anything else we should know?" said Frank. Brandi shook her head and blew her nose. Frank folded his notebook and said, "Are you ready to take a look?"

"Not really, but I guess..."

"That's what we're here for," said Leah.

"I know." Brandi grabbed her friend's hand. "Can she come with me?"

"If that's what you both want."

"It'll be okay," Brandi said, biting her lip again. "It's probably not him anyway."

Frank spoke to another intercom, and an inside door was opened by a white-coated attendant who ushered them into a freezing-cold room. Benny told the man who they wanted to see, but it seemed that he already knew what they were there for. Probably the place didn't get a lot of visitors.

If Brandi had been hoping to see someone other than Tony lying on the slab, she was bitterly disappointed. There was not going to be a holiday wedding. There was not going to be any wedding at all for Tony and Brandi.

CHAPTER SIX

I arrived at work on Monday and was immediately confronted by my boss, Marge Elliot.

"Tracy, when are you doing that interview out at Camp Kobmoosa?" Marge was the editor at the *Shagoni River News*. I had worked there for three years but some days she still managed to surprise me by the unflattering ensembles she wore to work. And this was one of those days. In deference to the hot weather, Marge had donned a sleeveless yellow dress with a big ruffle around the hips. Believe me, Marge does not need anything to accent her bottom, but there it was, graced by a macramé belt.

Before I could answer, Marge said, "You haven't forgotten about it, have you?"

"This morning," I said. "I've got it all set up."

"Well, good. You can take Holly with you. She'll be taking photos."

I tried, but failed, to suppress a groan. I had been looking forward to my morning away from the office, but the thought of taking a passenger changed everything. Especially this passenger.

I had first encountered Holly when she was in high school and taking a work/study class. Because of her interest in journalism, Holly had spent one afternoon per week at our office, sometimes going out into the field with a member of our staff. When she graduated, I thought I had seen the last of her, but no such luck—she had applied for a summer job. Marge had obliged her with the title of intern and was paying her a pittance to be a general gofer.

"I thought Kyle was going to take Holly today," I said. Kyle was young and, more importantly, male, and he seemed to think that dealing with Holly's chatter was a fair exchange for the occasional glimpse of a pierced naval or thong underwear.

"Change of plans," was all the explanation Marge was willing to offer. "I told her to be ready to go with you at nine o'clock."

And for once Holly was on time—wearing that red-and-white T-shirt that made her look like a hospital candy striper. She was equipped with the staff camera and was as talkative as ever.

"So, what's the name of this place we're going? And how far is it? Marge wants me back in the office by one, though I don't have any idea what for. And boy, I feel lucky that I get to be with you this morning, Ms. Quinn. This is going to be fun. Believe me, I had enough of Larry in the graphics room yesterday."

Holly and I were in my Honda on our way to do the interview. When she stopped for breath, I answered one of her many questions. "We're going to Camp Kobmoosa. Have you ever been a camper there?"

"Nope, never have—but I've heard all about it."

"What have you heard?"

"It's a place where rich people from Chicago send their kids—so the parents can go on vacation without them. My friend Andrea has a cousin who went there. And she said when campers get up in the morning, they have to jump in the lake before they can have breakfast."

"Ouch! I like swimming, but I don't think I'd want to do it before breakfast."

"Andrea said the counselors—well, they're college kids, mostly. And some of the guys are really cute. So, what's the name of this person we're going to meet?"

"Dallas something," I said. "Dallas Bursley, I think."

"Is that a man or a woman?"

"Good question. The fact is that I don't know...but we're going to find out soon."

****

I found the camp entrance and drove through a forest of pine and birch until I located the director's office, which was housed in a well-maintained log building. When I arrived, the director appeared on the front porch of the building to meet us.

Dallas Bursley turned out to be a woman—a woman on the far side of forty with wire-rimmed glasses and grey hair pulled back into a severe ponytail. After introductions, we followed her inside to a room with a huge stone fireplace. The walls were hung with posters that featured trees and bugs and flowers, and a few that suggested ways to prevent forest fires.

But once we were inside Bursley's office, the décor was strictly business, with desk, phone, computer, printer and file cabinets. It could have been an office anywhere in any city. She took a seat behind her desk and waved Holly and me into a pair of wooden chairs. We talked for a while about the long history of the camp, and Bursley told me that many of their campers came back as adults to vacation in the area. Eventually I asked about her previous work experience.

"My background is business and marketing," she said, "so when the board hired me, it represented a major change in philosophy. The camp's been around for over sixty years, and all the previous directors had degrees in outdoor education or something along that line."

"So your job is to change things up a little?" I wondered if the camp had been losing money.

She must have read my mind because she said, "We're still solvent, but attendance was starting to slide, so my mandate is to become more relevant—to slip some computer classes into the woods-and-water stuff. Also we're going to try..." Bursley paused, her attention diverted by a dark-haired young man who appeared in the doorway.

"Oh, sorry," he said. "I didn't realize you were busy."

"That's okay," she replied. "Ladies, this is my assistant Joel. Joel, these are visitors from the local newspaper."

"Pleased to meet you both." He flashed a smile in our direction. "I'll come back later."

"Okay," she said. "No, wait, Joel, don't leave. We can save some time. Why don't you take—is it Holly?—take Holly here for a little tour of the camp while Tracy and I finish up."

"But I'm supposed to take your picture," Holly blurted.

"Oh, no way," the director said emphatically. "No photo shoot today. Here, I'll give you something you can use instead." She pulled open a drawer and took out a brown envelope. "This is recent. It's the one I used for my application here." She held out the envelope until I finally took it, and that seemed to settle the matter.

"You take Holly and go ahead," she said to Joel. "She can get some shots of the staff. I think the lifeguards are having a meeting down by the channel."

Holly's expression showed that she was confused by the conflicting orders but also suggested that she was mesmerized by Joel and ready to follow him anywhere. I figured I could finish the interview without her. "You go right ahead," I said. "I'll meet you outside when I'm finished."

Dallas Bursley glanced at her watch as Holly and Joel departed.

"So your campers now have optional computer classes," I said. "What other changes are you planning for this season?"

"I suppose it's a sign of the times," she said with a sigh, "but we have a new staff position; it's a night watchman and he's on duty every night."

"Have there been problems?"

"Nothing too serious. Last summer a pair of counselors took a joy ride in a staff car. And when we did inventory this spring, a couple of kayaks were missing."

"Really? That's too bad."

"Yes, it's too bad that kayaking has become so popular. I'm told that no one has ever stolen a canoe."

"Guess they're too heavy to carry," I said, and we both chuckled. "Well, I think I've got plenty of material here. Is there anything else you'd like to tell me?"

"No, that's about it. But, if I may turn the tables, I'd like to ask you a question."

"Sure, go ahead."

"I understand that a body was found on the beach not far from here. Can you tell me anything about that?"

CHAPTER SEVEN

"Well, at least now we've got a name for the body," the sheriff said to Frank.

"Yep, we've got a name—Anthony, better known as Tony, Braxton."

"So now all we have to figure out is how he got from Big Rapids to being dead on our beach."

"We know there was water in his lungs," said Frank, "which is a clear indication of drowning. Plus, there was alcohol in his bloodstream."

"Which is pretty normal for a young man on a Saturday night."

"True...but we don't know why he was stripped down to his skivvies."

"Maybe he went for a swim."

"So we need to find his clothes. Are we sure he went in on Saturday night?"

"Close as Doc Marlin could guess," said the sheriff. "We got the body to the morgue on Tuesday, and he estimates it had been in the water somewhere over forty-eight hours."

The two men were in Frank's car this time, Benny's cruiser being in for repairs. They were on their way to visit George Antonelli, the man from Chicago who had discovered the body on his beach and called 911.

"Does this guy know we're coming?" said Benny.

"Yes, he does. Remember when we were out here retrieving the body? He was trying to be cooperative, but his dog was going crazy—"

"Oh yeah, we had to ask him to put the dog on a leash."

"Right. And then at the end he said he was heading back to Chicago in a few days. So I had to convince him—well, I sort of ordered him—to stick around until we could talk to him again. Said he would be leaving this afternoon. Is this where I turn?"

"Yep. Take a left up this hill and into the woods."

"Is it that big yellow house we saw from the road?'

"That's it."

Frank made another turn among the pine trees before their destination came into view, a large stucco building situated on the top of a dune.

"It might be interesting to see his house," Benny continued. "It's been here since the twenties and the story is that it was built by some big city gangsters."

"What were gangsters doing around here?"

"Smuggling in booze from Chicago."

"Smuggling? Oh, it was prohibition."

"Makes sense, doesn't it? Pleasure boats used to come up here from Chicago all the time."

Frank wanted to ask more questions about the gangsters but didn't have time because, as soon as he parked behind the cream colored house, a boisterous dog burst out of the back door to greet them. The dog was followed by a solidly built man dressed in a polo shirt and khaki pants.

"Come on in," said the man, "and don't mind Murphy—she gets a little excited when we have company."

Antonelli calmed the dog and escorted his visitors inside, leading them through an old-timey kitchen that was redolent with the smell of fresh coffee. They entered a dining room, which featured a stone fireplace and a wall of windows that offered a stunning view of Lake Michigan.

"Wonderful sight, isn't it?" said their host, gesturing to the lake, which was calm except for a few whitecaps. "That's why we bought the place. We updated the plumbing and electric but tried to leave everything else pretty much like it was. Can I get you some coffee or a beer—or Coke? I come and go, so I don't keep much fresh food here, but I always have some drinks and pretzels."

"Coffee sounds great," said Frank, and Benny nodded agreement.

Minutes later the three men were seated at the table with steaming cups of coffee and the promised bowl of pretzels. Murphy had settled under the table, announcing her presence only by the occasional thump of her tail. Benny began by telling their host that the body had now been identified.

"We know you found the body on Tuesday morning," said Frank as he pulled a small notebook out of his pocket. "Any idea as to when it showed up?"

"It must have arrived during the night. I had walked the beach the evening before—just about sunset. Everything was normal then."

"Is there much foot traffic on the beach?" said Benny.

"Only a few people on the weekends. Technically, the beach down there is mine, but Michigan law says that anyone can walk along the lake...that's fine with me."

"Any problems with the neighbors?"

"I get along with everybody—though I don't see much of them. As you can see, I'm pretty isolated. And all these lake properties are second homes...so people are here for weekends and maybe a week or two in the summer. The place is pretty empty after Labor Day. That's when the local kids come out to have bonfires on the beach. We know that because we find the remains of their fires. I don't mind the parties, though it does aggravate me when they steal my firewood. But they only take what's outside. If I lock it up, they go somewhere else."

"How long have you had this place?" said Frank.

"We bought it about ten years ago, wanted a summer getaway...a place for the grandkids to come and visit. It's worked out really well..." Antonelli paused, cleared his throat. "My wife died...two years ago, so it's not the same. Now it's just me and Murphy."

On hearing her name, the dog stirred and thumped her tail.

"Okay, girl," he said. "We'll get another walk before we leave. Is there anything else?'

"You said you are retired," said Frank. "What did you do when you were working?"

Antonelli seemed to consider his answer. "I was in the investment business...still am, on a consultant basis." He finished his coffee. "Anything else you'd like to know?"

Benny looked at Frank, who shrugged. "That's it for now."

"Well good," said Antonelli. "Okay if I ask a question now?"

"We'll answer if we can," said Frank.

"What's your best guess on how the body got to my beach?"

"It happened in one of two ways," said Frank. "Either the victim went in somewhere along the shoreline or he came off a boat."

"Ever find any clothes?"

"No, not yet. That would help us a lot."

"I suppose somebody could have drowned him and dragged the body to the beach," said the sheriff, "but that seems like a lot of work."

"I agree," said Antonelli. Then he glanced at his watch. "If that's it, I need to get going. Murphy and I are going to walk the beach before I leave. Care to join us? It's only eighty-nine steps down."

"Tempting," said Benny, "but we'd better move on. And could you give us a phone number, in case anything comes up?'

"Sure," said Antonelli. He located his wallet, extracted a business card, and handed it to the sheriff. "I'll walk out with you. There's a loose board in that landing I've been meaning to fix."

As they negotiated the back porch steps, Frank saw a pair of kayaks, one orange and one red, leaning against the outer wall of the garage.

"Do you kayak?" he said.

"I haven't tried it yet," said Antonelli. "Those belong to my son."

"Well, thanks for the coffee," said the sheriff, "and have a good trip back to Chicago."

After they were in the car and making their way down the winding driveway, Frank said, "Didn't he seem a little vague about his business?"

"I bet he's a lawyer," said Benny.

"What does his card say?"

Benny pulled Antonelli's business card from his shirt pocket and looked it over. "Got his name, two phone numbers, email, website. P.O. box, but no physical address—says he's a business consultant."

"I bet you're right," said Frank. "Lawyers tend to be vague."

"Lawyers and politicians," said Benny. "Where do we go next?"

"Another visit out this way. I think I know how to find this one." Ten minutes later Frank was parking in a dirt lot next to a hedge of juniper and pine when he was surprised to see a familiar face.

"Tracy Quinn," he said, as he climbed out. "What on earth are you doing here?"

"Well, hello, Frank—and you too, Benny," said Tracy. "I just finished an interview...but I might ask you the same question. What is the long arm of the law doing out at Camp Kobmoosa?"

CHAPTER EIGHT

"Those two cops we met," said Holly. "Was that one guy your boyfriend?"

"I suppose that's what you would call him," I said, once again wishing there was a more age-appropriate word for mature people who were in some degree of relationship. I had tried them all. *Companion* sounded like a pet. *Best friend* sounded a little adolescent. *Gentleman friend* sounded pretentious. So *boyfriend* it was. I hastened to change the subject.

"How was your time with Joel? Did you get any photos?"

"Oh yeah. He was great...we talked to the life guards and swim instructors, and I took some pictures of them all down by the water."

"I can't guarantee we'll use them."

"I know. Because Marge specifically wanted a photo of the new director. But I wonder why Dallas Bursley wouldn't let me take her picture?"

"Me too. Her reaction seemed a little bit strange, didn't it?"

"Maybe she was having a bad hair day."

Holly and I were having lunch at Cherry Point Farm market—my treat, of course. I guess hunger had overcome my aversion to the girl's company...or maybe lunch with Holly seemed like the lesser evil compared to facing Marge and explaining the photo difficulty. She would blame me, of course.

But Holly didn't seem to be worried about anything. "Look at this," she said. "Joel gave me a T-shirt." She produced a rolled-up piece of cloth and shook it out for my inspection.

The shirt was red and featured that overused logo—a dream catcher—with the name of the camp emblazoned around it. "You favorite color," I said.

"Not only that, but he invited me to an open house at camp next week. Want to go with me?"

"Hmm. That all depends—on my calendar. But hey, it sounds like you two hit it off pretty well."

"He sure is cute, isn't he?"

"Pretty nice to look at," I agreed, while thinking that if Joel's job description included public relations, he was doing well in that area.

"Ms. Quinn." Holly paused, holding half of her sandwich in the air.

"Call me Tracy."

"Okay, Tracy. I wonder if I could ask you for—some advice?"

I really wanted to say no. The last time Holly had asked me for advice, she had been dealing with evidence that pointed to her father having an affair. I hoped that was not erupting again because I'm no good at this stuff. But of course I didn't say that. I took a drink, swallowed hard, and said, "Okay go ahead."

"It's about this guy that I like and well, I'm pretty sure he'd like to ask me out... but there's a problem."

"A problem – like what?"

She twisted her straw while she explained. "Umm well, he was going with a friend of mine until they broke up...about two weeks ago. And I don't want her to be mad at me. What do you think I should do?"

I thought for a moment. "Two weeks isn't very long," I said, "so he's probably on the rebound. But if you really don't want to hurt your girlfriend, why not just ask her if she would mind?"

"Okay, that makes sense. I guess I've been sort of avoiding her ...and things have been a little weird. And thank you, Tracy. It really helps me to talk to someone like you—you know—an older person."

Thanks a lot for that, kid.

On the way back to town I took my time. Mainly because I was in no hurry to face Marge, but also because a wind was gusting out of the west and I had a little trouble keeping my Honda on the road. It was after one thirty when we got back to the office. Sylvia was at the front desk and said, "Marge wants to see you right away."

"Sure," I replied. "Is that me or Holly?"

"I'm not sure. She just said to send her the next person who walked in the door."

Marge met us in the hallway. "You need to get over to the state park," she said. "The park manager just called 911."

"Sure," I said. "What's the crisis?"

"Near as we could tell, they've got a missing swimmer."

****

It took me less than five minutes to reach the state park. Holly was with me since Marge had not given her any other instructions, but I told her to leave the camera in the car. I parked in a handicapped spot, figuring my status as a member of the press should offer some advantage in case anybody challenged me.

"Gosh," said Holly, "I've never seen the beach like this before."

The beach was usually dotted with sun bathers on lounge chairs and blankets –but not today. The sky was filling with dark clouds, sand was swirling, kids were crying and parents were busy packing up their gear.

"I saw it like this once before," I said as we approached the beach. "And that was just before a twister."

"Look at the flag," she said.

The current beach flag was red...indicating no one should be in the water. A couple of teen agers were ignoring that warning, but mainly a full-scale exodus was in process, with people heading for their cars or the campground. I looked around for somebody in authority but wasn't having any luck. I decided to try the camp store, where I found a pair of teenage girls behind the counter, one dipping ice cream and the other grilling a hot dog. Pushing to the front of the line, I said, "Excuse me, but I need to speak to the park manager."

"That would be Mr. Swanson?"

"Yes, do you know where he is?"

"No." She looked at the other girl. "Tiffany, do you know where Mr. Swanson is?"

The ice cream girl shrugged. "Haven't seen him since about ten this morning...that's when he comes in to, you know, check on us."

For some reason, this sent them both into fits of giggling. I thanked the girls and left the store, the wind banging the door behind me. I was trying to decide what to do next when Holly approached me and said, "Ms. Quinn—um, Tracy—that girl out by your car—isn't she the one that's, ah, staying with you?"

I looked to where Holly was pointing and recognized the brown-clad figure of Brooke. She must have been coming from the campground but now had stopped in the parking lot where she seemed to be taking an interest in my car. With Holly trailing close behind, I hurried out to confront my ex-stepdaughter, whose hair had escaped from its braid and was blowing about in the wind.

"Hey, girl," I said. "That car is privileged."

"Oh, Tracy," she replied. "I thought it looked like yours. Don't worry, I don't have authority to give out tickets anyway."

"That's good. Otherwise you might be looking for a new place to sleep tonight."

She laughed and tried to smooth down her hair. "Oh, that would never happen."

"Marge sent us over," I said. "Is it true you have a swimmer missing?"

Brooke's expression turned serious. "Somebody is definitely missing," she said. "It's a twelve-year-old girl who was camping here with her mom and her aunt. The mom reported this a little while ago. The girl, her name is Lexie, left before noon. She told her mother she was going for a swim and headed for the beach. And they haven't seen her since."

"Is she a good swimmer?"

"Pretty good, I guess. On her junior high swim team. I was just over at the campsite with Mr. Swanson. The mom is getting hysterical. We walked over to the lake, but there was nobody on the beach at all. And you know how the waves wipe out footprints in a minute so..."

We all looked out at the water, where whitecaps were forming under the darkening sky. A fat drop of rain splattered on my arm.

"It doesn't sound good, does it?"

"No, it doesn't," Brooke said. "Jerry Louter, the cop, came out and talked to Mr. Swanson, and they both went down to the village marina. I think they were going to go out in the police boat to see if they could find her."

The three of us stood and looked out over Lake Michigan as the rain moved in. I wondered if this was going to mean two drownings in one week. I thought about the headline: *Lake Michigan Claims Another Victim.* (Sorry if that seems ghoulish, but I am, after all, a reporter.) At the same time, the vision of another body washing up on our shoreline made me feel both angry and helpless.

"But then," said Brooke, "when the mom quit crying, she told us something else."

"What was that?"

"She said she's going through a divorce and she's afraid—she's afraid maybe—that the girl's dad came and took her."

CHAPTER NINE

After an overnight storm the weather cleared, leaving the air with a freshly washed smell. On Saturday evening I drove out to Frank's cabin, a neat little A-frame about ten miles north of town. He had invited me for dinner. "I'm glad you could get away from town," said Frank as he filled my bowl with his secret recipe venison stew.

"I am too," I said. "Sometimes things get a little busy at my house—what with Brooke and Derek and their new friend. The two of them are both spending time with this guy named Scott. Remember him?"

"How could I forget? The peach pie was great."

We were sitting at the picnic table outside Frank's cabin, where we could hear the babble of the Shagoni River through a thick border of willow and cedar trees. "How long before Derek goes back to Arizona?" he wondered.

"One more week. Sometimes I think Scott is just waiting to make a move on Brooke."

"Speaking of Brooke, I heard there was some excitement out at the state park."

"Oh, the missing swimmer," I said. "Yeah, that had our undies in a bunch for a while."

"But the girl was okay?"

"She was fine. Her cousin found her at the House of Flavors sharing a Pig's Dinner banana split. The girl wasn't even wet—because she never went in the lake."

"So why did she say she was going swimming?"

"Mainly to throw her family off track. She had a date—with one of our own."

"A local?"

"Yep an older man. He was fifteen." Frank had a good laugh. "Aren't you glad you don't have children?"

"Most of the time, yes, I am."

"That mother's got a busy time ahead of her. Want some more stew?"

Frank's venison stew was an acquired taste, but in the course of two years in his company, I had learned to enjoy it. "Sure, I'll have some more."

When he returned with my refill, I said, "I've been thinking about that body on the beach—what was the young man's name?"

"Tony, Tony Braxton."

"Tony must have had a car. Why hasn't an abandoned vehicle showed up anywhere?"

"I agree. A guy that age usually has a car. Benny and I were interested in a burned-out vehicle that was found near Saugatuck."

"Burned- out would definitely indicate foul play."

"True...but that was before we talked to the girlfriend again...she explained that Tony was temporarily without wheels. Seems he had a nice little Mustang but had totaled it."

"When did that happen?"

"A week or two before he died, and he had not replaced it...she said there was a problem with his insurance."

"Like maybe he had neglected to pay the premium?"

"Yep, that usually happens right before an accident. Do you want that last biscuit?"

"Go ahead."

"But there was one other interesting piece of news," Frank said as he reached for the honey. "This was from the postmortem. They found Flexeril in his bloodstream."

****

"Flexeril," I repeated, trying to recall what I knew about the drug. "So our victim had ingested a prescription drug. How high was the level?"

"Fairly high," said Frank. "Certainly more than a therapeutic dose."

"I know the stuff is a muscle relaxant," I said. "I'm pretty sure I took some once."

"Sure. Most of us have, at one time or another."

"Mine was for a strained shoulder. I remember it laid me flat on my back for half a day...I never took any more of it."

"It tends to affect people differently. I took some, and it didn't do a thing for me."

"That's because you're so big and tough." I gave him an affectionate shove. "But how do you think it might have affected—Tony?"

"For one thing, it probably made it a lot harder for him to swim."

"Do you think someone gave it to him deliberately?"

"We're trying not to jump to conclusions," said Frank. "I asked the girlfriend if he was taking any prescription medication, and she said nothing that she knew of."

"Was he living with this girlfriend?"

"Sounds like he was at her place, mostly—then, if they weren't getting along, he crashed with some guy friends till things straightened out."

I slapped at a mosquito. "Frank, I love the great outdoors but I think maybe it's time to move inside." We cleared up the remains of our meal and moved inside. Frank got busy starting a fire in the fireplace. But I kept thinking about the drowning victim.

"So this Tony...have you talked to his parents?"

"Not yet. They're both teachers who recently retired, and they went on an extended trip to celebrate. I think the bad news caught up with them somewhere in Australia. So they're cutting the trip short. They should be back sometime this week."

"There's another thing I wonder about. Why were you and Benny out at Camp Kobmoosa on Friday?"

"We were just nosing around, mostly. Given that the body was found not too far north of there."

"I suppose Dallas Bursley was glad to see you, in a way. She had just asked me what I knew about the body on the beach."

"What did you tell her?" Frank grabbed a poker and rearranged the logs on the fire.

"I told her I didn't know any more than what she had already read in the newspaper."

"Naturally she asked us the same question," said Frank. "And I did tell her the victim's name."

"I can see why she would be curious about the body. I didn't realize quite how close to the camp the body was found."

"On the plat map it's just over one mile."

"As the sea gull flies," I said. "But tell me, what was your impression of Bursley?"

"Certainly businesslike—pleasant enough, but also maybe a little guarded."

"That's to be expected I guess. She certainly doesn't want to see the death connected with the camp."

"I got that impression too," said Frank. "She stressed that the young man had no connection to the camp."

"But there was one thing about her that seemed strange. She wouldn't let Holly take her photo."

"Did she give any reason?"

"Nope." We were quiet for a bit, watching the fire. Then I had an idea. "If you'd like to talk to some other people at the camp," I said, "there's going to be an event there on Tuesday evening that's open to the public."

"What kind of event?"

"Near as I can tell, it's an open house for prospective campers, parents, and so on. Plus, a talk on the history of the area, with a plug for the environment."

Frank was quiet for a moment before he answered. "Sounds good, but it doesn't work for me. I've got an all-day meeting in Detroit and there's no way I could get back in time."

"Well, darn, I was hoping we could go together."

"But what about you? Why don't you go out and mingle? It'll give you a chance to talk with staff other than Bursley. And you are very good at listening to conversations."

"Sometimes called eavesdropping."

"No law against that." He stood and took a jacket from a peg by the door.

"What do you say we walk up the hill and see if we can catch the moonrise?"

"Sounds good to me."

"And did you say you could spend the night?"

"I think that is a very good idea."

CHAPTER TEN

I was tempted to sneak off to the open house at Camp Kobmoosa by myself, but that didn't happen, mainly because Holly spent most of the day Monday reminding me about it and wanting to know if I was planning to go. I stalled as long as possible but, around noon the next day, I finally caved.

"Yes, I'm going," I said. "And you can come along if you like."

"Oh great. Thanks, Ms. Quinn—I mean, Tracy."

Since Frank had more or less sent me on a snooping mission, I would have preferred to go alone, but I realized it was only fair for me to take Holly, considering that she was the one who had snagged the invitation.

Tuesday evening found me in the main dining hall of the camp with a name tag on my shirt, holding a cup of punch in one hand and a plate of crackers in the other, while I scanned the table for cheesecake or brownies. If there had been any such offerings, the early guests had eliminated them in a hurry.

I estimated the crowd at about fifty people, divided among potential campers (young, bored—probably ate all the brownies), parents of potential campers (my age), and counselors (college age). I needn't have worried about Holly being any kind of impediment because, shortly after her arrival, I saw her talking to Joel, the guy who had provided her with the camp T-shirt and also the event invitation. Shortly afterward, both of them disappeared from my radar.

So I did as Frank had suggested –I mingled. First I made a point of speaking to Dallas Bursley, who was dressed in khaki-colored slacks and shirt, which actually looked kind of chic because the material was some shiny synthetic.

Plus, she wore gold hoop earrings and her hair was piled on top of her head.

Bursley clearly remembered me, because she wanted to know when my story about the camp would appear in the paper. I said soon. She asked if she could review the article first, and I said that was not our policy but I would mention her request to my editor. I was sure that Marge would make short work of her.

The next person I recognized was Morton Fitzgerald, the county commissioner whose district included the camp and surrounding area. Fitzgerald is about five seven with big ears and round glasses, and his appearance always makes me think of a mouse, but I like the guy and have always found him easy to talk to.

"Hi, Mort," I said, "good to see you."

"Tracy," he replied. "What brings you out this way?"

"Just the cheese and crackers, I guess. How about you? Is this a regular event for you?"

"To tell the truth," he said, "I've been invited every year, but this is the first time I ever made the effort to attend."

"Well, good for you," I said. "Any special reason?"

"Yes, there is, in fact. Let's go over there." Mort nodded toward a less-populated corner of the room. I followed him to an alcove that featured a coat rack and a stack of folding chairs.

"First of all," he said when he had determined that no one was paying us any attention, "you should know that this camp is prime real estate."

"I hadn't thought about it that way," I said, which was true. Then I pictured the camp as two hundred acres of undisturbed trees, sea grass, and dunes lying between Lake Michigan and Stoney Lake. "But yes, now that you mention it, I can see that it would be."

"Every few years some developer from Chicago or Saugatuck comes nosing around. They consider this area underdeveloped."

"Because it's not yet covered with buildings and sidewalks?"

"That's about it."

"It's not for sale, is it?"

"No, and so far, never has been."

"But now?"

"There's been talk from one of these groups about acquiring just a portion of the camp property, possibly a few acres on the south part of the beach. The developers want to build a couple of condos, or maybe half a dozen duplexes."

"What's your position on that?"

"That's what I'm trying to decide. Of course the boost in property tax would be welcome, but there is a downside."

"And what is that?"

"What happens is that people from the city buy out here, and they don't understand what they're getting into. Then, all of a sudden, they want better bridges, more policing, faster internet, and someone to plow their roads in the winter."

Mort Fitzgerald and I were still talking when the speaker of the evening was announced. So we left off our conversation to join the audience. The woman was from the Michigan Wildlife Commission, and she was trying to present an overview of how the camp fit into the area. I probably didn't give her the attention she deserved because I was thinking about the information I had just acquired from Fitzgerald about the possible sale of part of the camp.

The news gave me a little more insight into Dallas Bursley's position. If the camp was bleeding money, then selling off a few acres of waterfront would be a tempting solution—but it would drastically change the nature of the area. So it was Bursley's job to avoid that possibility by making the camp more profitable. Suddenly I had more respect for the woman.

As soon as the speaker had finished, Bursley took the podium, where she thanked us for coming and made it clear that the event was over. Fortunately, Holly had reappeared by then, so I didn't have to go looking for her.

On the way home Holly thanked me profusely for taking her, babbled about her friend Joel and all the cool kids she had met and how she was going to apply to work at camp next summer. I was only half listening when she said something that caught my attention.

"Joel introduced me to the night watchman," she said. "His name is Mickey something. He looked Hispanic, but no accent."

I hadn't seen anyone of that description. "Was this person at the open house?"

"No, we were outside. Mickey seemed to be checking the cars in the parking lot."

"Guess he wasn't important enough to be inside."

"Maybe not. But he was kind of nice looking." She giggled. "And later on Joel told me something else about him."

"What was that?"

"Joel said Mickey got the job because he's dating the camp director."

****

Things were quiet at work the next day, so I went home at noon and made a grilled cheese sandwich. Seated at the kitchen table, I poured a glass of lemonade and took a bite of sandwich, which was crunchy and gooey all at once. That's when I heard Brooke coming downstairs.

"Morning, Tracy."

I hadn't realized that my housemate was home but, with her rotating work schedule, her presence—or absence—was never a total surprise. "I think we are well past noon," I said, "but good morning anyway. I didn't know you were home."

She opened the fridge and secured a glass of orange juice before she sat down across from me. I thought she was looking a little bleary eyed.

"Is this your day off?" I said.

"I'm not sure—but I hope so."

After three summers with Brooke, I generally made a point of treating her as an adult and avoided taking on any kind of mother role, so I tried to keep my next comment from carrying any hint of judgment.

"Guess you had a late night?"

"You might say that. First of all, I worked second shift. Got done at nine. Then Derek and Scott came by to see if I wanted to go with them to the casino."

"In Manistee?"

"Right. Well, I had never been. Scott said it was free to walk in and we didn't have to gamble if we didn't want to—we could just look around. So we decided we'd give it a try. We went in Scott's car and walked in. But the rest of it didn't work out quite the way I expected."

"How so?"

"After we got inside, we kind of split up. I just walked around and gawked at everything, but the two guys got involved with the slot machines—I guess they pretty much lost all their cash. It was after midnight when we met up again, and they told me they were broke. I figured it was time to go home—I had enough money to buy gas, if that's what we needed. But then Scott had this big idea about going to some club he had heard about—a place called the Silver Slipper that had an all-girl rock band."

"I've heard of it," I said. I had also heard was that it was a low life place frequented by drug dealers and their patrons. But I didn't say anything about that.

Brooke continued. "I said if we were so broke we should just go home, and Derek was ready to go too. But Scott said no, he had seen an ATM machine and he would get us some cash. Scott was driving, so he pretty much got his way. He went to the ATM and took out—looked like at least a couple hundred dollars. We left there, and then he got lost trying to find the bar, so it was late when we finally found it and I was really tired. But Scott insisted we go inside, so I had a beer and watched some trashy-looking girls play their last set."

"How was the music?"

"Okay I guess. By then I just wanted to be home, so I wasn't paying much attention. We got home late, and we were all a little cranky."

"So that was you I heard stumbling in about three this morning?"

"That was me. Hope I didn't wake you."

"Not for long."

She took a long swallow of her juice. "But you know, thinking about it this morning, I wonder—sometimes I wonder why Scott feels the need to spend so much money. Maybe it's because— "

"Because he's trying to impress you?"

"Possibly. But then I wonder why he has so much money to throw around in the first place. Remember, he told us he just finished college."

"I remember—that night he had supper with us. Said he spent so much fixing his car that he couldn't afford to take a road trip."

"Right. That's why he ended up coming to work for his uncle."

"Can't be much money in tossing around watermelons—but hey, it's worked out well for us. Frank still raves about your peach pie."

"I don't think Scott would be stealing from his relatives, do you?"

"I doubt if there's much cash around for him to steal."

Brooke glanced at the clock, and her expression turned serious. She groaned and ran fingers through her hair. "I am working today and I need to be there in half an hour."

"Good luck with that," I said as I cleared away my lunch and got up to leave. "There's an enchilada in the refrigerator."

"I was thinking—I seem to remember a piece of chocolate cake."

"Cake for breakfast?" I said, trying to quell the judgmental tone that was creeping into my voice.

"I think I just need some quick energy."

I took a deep breath and recalibrated. "Chocolate cake would be a good source of energy," I said, remembering my misspent youth.

CHAPTER ELEVEN

Frank called me the next morning and I took the call, despite Marge's rule about no personal phone calls at work. I figured that since Frank is a county official, I could always justify our conversations as part of my job. (We do make an effort to limit the sweet talk, which is not difficult since Frank is not a sweet talk kind of guy.) "Did you get out to the camp last night?" he said.

"Yes I did. Holly and I—"

"Did you learn anything?"

"Maybe. The county commissioner, Mort Fitzgerald, was there, and he told me he's heard talk about possible sale and development of part of the camp property—just rumors at this point."

"That would certainly meet some opposition. Locals are protective of their waterfront. Was there anything specific?"

"The only thing I recall is that the developers were out of Chicago."

"That figures. Anything else?"

"Let's see. Holly said she met the night watchman."

"Do you think the guy was on duty on Saturday two weeks ago?"

"Maybe. I guess the night watchman should be on duty every night."

"Do you have a name for this guy?"

"Miguel something—they call him Mickey."

"Good work. I think I'll swing by the camp and see if I can find this Mickey. I've got a meeting now, so I gotta go. Is it okay if I come by tonight with something for supper?"

That was the moment Marge walked in. "I think that would work, Mr.

Kolowsky, do call me about the details." I doubt if Frank even picked up on the difference in my tone. But he should have figured it out. After all, he's a detective.

Frank showed up at my house as promised. It was shortly after six when I got home and found him waiting on my porch swing—the swing squeaked and groaned as he stood and gave me a perfunctory kiss. "We need to get some oil on those hinges," he said.

"Don't hurry with that," I replied. "The squeak reminds me of when I was a little girl. I spent hours in the swing when my mother and I came here to visit."

"Okay. We'll save the squeak. I got some corned beef sandwiches from that new deli in town." He brandished a paper bag. "Hope that's okay."

"You know I like corned beef."

"Trouble is, I didn't get any for Brooke. Sort of forgot about her being here
"

"That's not a problem," I said as we moved inside. "I don't see a whole lot of Brooke, and we don't normally eat together unless we make some kind of appointment."

"Everything okay—with you and Brooke?"

"Sure, no problem there. It's just that she tends to keep very busy with a full-time job and two young men in her life."

"Two? Is one of them Derek?"

"Yes, and the other is a guy named Scott. Remember the kid that brought us all the peaches and cherries?"

"How could I forget that peach pie?"

In the kitchen, Frank and I talked while we set out condiments ranging from mustard and horseradish to coleslaw and dill pickles. I poured us some water and, with very little ceremony, we sat down and dug in. "This is good—and the sandwich has real sauerkraut," I said while retrieving a string of the kraut that was threatening to escape.

"Glad you like it."

I was reaching for the horseradish when I had a thought. "Hey, I just made a connection—about that business out on the lake."

"Let's hear it."

"Mort Fitzgerald said the potential developers were out of Chicago." Frank nodded, his mouth full. "Well, that guy who found the body—what was his name?"

"Something Italian—Antonelli."

"Okay. Well, isn't Mr. Antonelli from Chicago?"

"Yes he is," said Frank. "But I wouldn't read too much into that. I bet that half of those big houses on the lake are owned by people from Chicago. No one who lives and works in this county has that kind of money."

"Okay, so much for my Chicago connection theory."

"Sorry to shoot it down. But please, don't let me discourage any other ideas on your part. Right now we're pretty much open to any suggestions."

"Okay, I'll keep brainstorming."

"Do you want any more potato salad?"

"Nope, go ahead and take it. But tell me, did you talk with Mickey—the night watchman out at camp?"

"I did. Had to wake him up, but he didn't seem to mind."

"I guess it comes with working a night shift," I said. "You know, I'm a little surprised they added a new position while the camp is trying to economize."

"Mickey told me some kayaks had gone missing from camp."

"I remember Bursley said that too. But a night watchman would cost a lot more than a couple of kayaks —don't you think?"

"The kayaks were only part of it. Mickey said that some of the counselors had a habit of sneaking out during the night. Last year one guy helped himself to a camp vehicle and then had a fender-bender in the wee hours. The kid had no authority to be driving, so insurance didn't cover— "

"Okay, now the night watchman is making more sense. Did he tell you that Dallas Bursley is his lady friend?"

"No, that didn't come up," Frank said with a chuckle. "How about that coleslaw?"

"It's all yours. Anyway, did Mickey tell you anything else of interest?"

"As a matter of fact, he did. He said that on the night in question, he saw a bonfire on the beach around midnight."

"A bonfire usually means a beach party. Where was it?"

"He put it maybe half a mile north of the camp."

"Interesting. But how can he be so sure—about the date, I mean?"

"Part of Mickey's job is to keep a log of any unusual activity. So we checked his records, and there it was—he was walking the shoreline when he saw the bonfire."

"Did he investigate?"

"No, because it wasn't camp property. Also, it's pretty normal activity for a Saturday night in the summer."

"So, what do you think?"

"It could be nothing—but on the other hand, I'm wondering if there's any chance that our victim, Tony Braxton, might have been at that party."

"The timing seems right," I said. "What's your next step?"

"I'm going back out there tomorrow morning. Mickey and I are going to walk the beach and see what we can find."

****

My job the following day was to cover the county commissioners' meeting in Stanton, which meant meetings all day with a two-hour break for lunch. County board day also meant I had to deal with my friend Ivy, whether I wanted to or not, because Ivy Martin and I sit together at the press table.

Ivy is a reporter for the *Manistee Chronicle*, a daily paper forty miles to the north. I still remember the night we first met—I was new to my job, and we were both up late at the courthouse covering an election. On that occasion, Ivy was a big help to me on the job, and provided a measure of stress relief with her irreverent sense of humor.

But my friendship with Ivy had fractured later on when it was revealed that she had committed an indiscretion with Paul Lavallen, who happened to be married to my best friend, Jewell. Ivy swore it was only once and would never happen again. But after that I had never felt quite the same about her.

I suppose it didn't help matters when she had a fling with my ex-husband—although that was so long after our divorce it shouldn't have been a big deal for me—and it really wasn't. Still, I had balked at her requests for intimate advice about his personal habits and sexual preferences. Ivy seemed to have no boundaries.

Other than her predatory habits where men were concerned, there was another thing about Ivy that made me uneasy, though I told myself it was silly. That thing was her ability to look put together, stylish, and color-coordinated on any and all occasions, leaving me feeling like a bit of a klutz whenever we appeared together.

On this particular morning, I was alone at the press table while I listened to complaints about an unauthorized dog kennel, a subject which took up nearly an hour. Then, right around eleven thirty, Ivy Martin breezed in, wearing a blouse in a color I believe is called burnt orange, which contrasted nicely with the flowered scarf around her neck. Her long, dark hair was caught in a fancy double-comb arrangement. Her earrings were dangly bronze and the entire ensemble gave the impression of Egyptian nobility.

The county board was almost all men, and every one of their heads turned as Ivy made her late entrance. (Oh hell, even the female commissioner turned to look.) Ivy plunked down beside me and proceeded to spread her papers, notepad, pens, breath mints and other paraphernalia all over our table. "Did I miss anything?" she said in a loud whisper.

"Nothing important," I whispered back.

Ivy was quiet for a few minutes, hastily scribbling on her steno pad. But minutes later she leaned close and said, "When this is over, let's have lunch at Schooners. I've got news."

Although I usually tried to beg off on lunch dates with Ivy, she knew I had trouble resisting the promise of information. Sometimes her news was just idle gossip or a development in her love life—but at other times she had picked up a real tip from someone in the courthouse or city hall. Ivy definitely had her ways.

Half an hour later, the two of us walked out of the courthouse and headed to Schooners Bar, which was Ivy's first choice for lunch. It was a short walk from the courthouse, and I suspected that she enjoyed the presence of a largely male clientele. Ivy's favorite table was a tall one by a window that offered a good view and a measure of privacy. We found the table empty, although a trio of women were eyeing it as they tried to reach a group decision on where to sit.

Ivy ended their debate when she said, "Sorry, ladies, but I have this table reserved."

With that, she grabbed my arm and led me to the table in question. We climbed onto the tall chairs, looked over the menus and made small talk until the waitress took our orders.

Then I spoke up. "Ivy, you said you had news for me."

"I do, but let's wait until we get our food." She glanced around and added quietly, "We wouldn't want to get interrupted."

"Okay," I said, "but you act like you're sharing classified information."

"Maybe I am—ever think of that?"

The waitress delivered our food and, as soon as she was out of earshot, I tried again. "So, Ivy, what is this news you picked up?"

"Okay." She wiped her mouth, laid down her napkin and leaned forward. "Well, you probably know about the body on the beach."

"Of course. I've written two stories about it, including the one this week, which said it is now considered a suspicious death."

" And did you see the sheriff on Channel Three last night?"

"I guess I missed that."

"It was sort of a big deal. They're calling it the Cedar County Mystery Death. And I guess they gave the guy's name—although I've forgotten it."

"The name is Tony Braxton. He was from Big Rapids." So far, I felt like Ivy was doing the fishing and I was taking the bait.

"Well." Ivy glanced around, as though checking for surveillance. "I don't think this should be made public."

I ran my fingers across my lips with a zipping motion, all the while knowing I would make my own decision on how to use Ivy's big tip. If such a thing ever manifested. Finally it did.

"I saw the sheriff this morning," she whispered. "Benny told me they found the dead guy's clothes."

"Really?" I made an effort not to sound surprised.

"Yep, found the stuff right there on the beach."

"On the beach—where, exactly?"

"Not too far from that camp down there, the one with the funny name."

Ivy's revelation left me, literally, speechless. Her information may or may not have been accurate. But accurate or not, I didn't understand how Ivy had picked pick up this morsel before me—considering that I was the one who was sleeping with the county detective.

CHAPTER TWELVE

"I hear you found some clothes on the beach," I said to Frank, trying to sound casual.

"And how did you get that bit of news?" Was that a hint of hostility in his voice?

"From Ivy."

It was Friday evening, and Frank had come by to take me out to Paul and Jewell Lavallen's house for dinner. I had suggested that he come early so we could talk and have a glass of wine. So that's what we were doing, but the talk was not getting off to a very good start. I kept my tone neutral as I proceeded to explain. "I got this news from Ivy, who got it from Sheriff Benny Dupree, yesterday at the courthouse."

If I had thought the mood was becoming tense, Frank dispersed it all with his best belly laugh. "Your friend Ivy," he said, "sure knows her way around the male of the species."

"I guess she does."

"The funny thing is that Benny is always warning me about leaking information—because he thinks I talk too much with you about what goes on in his department. And then he blabs, to the biggest mouth in the county—who happens to also be a reporter."

"She probably just batted those eyelashes at him and said, 'What's new, Sheriff?'" I did my best imitation of Ivy's butterfly eyes. "But tell me—did someone actually find clothes on the beach?"

"She was right about that. Remember, I told you Mickey and I were going to walk the beach in the morning. So we did. First we found remnants of a campfire—and the remains were pretty close to a long flight of steps leading up to one of the cottages. The building was big, so it's really not a cottage."

"More of a beach house, I guess."

"Right. So then Mickey and I hiked up the steps to the beach house and knocked on the doors, but the place was empty. Finally we found a neighbor who said the owner's name was Max Merrifield and he lived in Reed City. He also confirmed that there were a whole lot of people around a week ago Saturday night."

"Will you go to Reed City and try to find this Mr. Merrifield?"

"I'm going to wait. The neighbor said he thought the guy was planning to be around this weekend."

"That makes sense. The weather's supposed to be fabulous." I refilled our wine glasses.

"So then Mickey and I went back to the beach and I asked him if he wanted to keep looking. He said sure—I think this whole thing was kind of exciting for him. We spread out and were both walking the dunes when he yelled to me. I went over and saw that he had stumbled on a pile of stuff almost covered up by sand. It turned out to be clothes."

"Beach stuff?"

"Guy stuff. Jeans and a T-shirt—plus running shoes and socks."

"Any identification?"

"Zilch. There was no wallet in the pants or any other ID."

"So it could have been anyone just going for a swim."

"Could have been." He paused for a drink. "But the T-shirt was black with a picture of some heavy metal band. I took a photo of the shirt and sent it to Brandi, Tony Braxton's girlfriend. Half an hour later she called back and said Tony had a T-shirt just like that—I don't know why she started crying. She already knew he was dead."

"Could have been a reminder. Maybe she gave him the shirt."

"Yeah, something like that."

"So it looks like you found out where Tony Braxton went into the water."

"Yep, now we just need to figure out why he didn't come out." Frank finished his wine and looked at his watch. "Guess we should get going."

"Right. We don't want to keep a good meal waiting. I think Paul caught some salmon."

"Wouldn't want to miss that."

We were in Frank's car, and I was getting buckled up when I said, "Frank, did you ever think that maybe Mickey knew something?"

"What do you mean?"

"What I mean is—did it seem like Mickey knew where to look for those clothes?"

Frank hesitated just a moment before he turned on the ignition. "You know," he said, "I hadn't thought about it that way."

******

"Did you remember to bring the wine?" Frank said as we pulled in to the driveway of Lavallen's house on Arrowhead Lake.

"Yes, I did." I produced the brown paper bag. "I believe that white goes with fish, but I'm afraid I didn't have time to get it very cold."

"I'm sure it will be fine, whatever temperature it is."

Within minutes of our arrival, the chardonnay was chilling in the freezer and Frank was down at the dock with Paul, looking over his fishing boat. I was on their deck setting the table, a task I enjoyed because it meant that I was immersed in the scent of pine and cedar trees.

To me, it was the scent of comfort because I had come to this house so many times feeling distraught and left feeling able to cope again. Now I was happy to be here when I was not struggling with a problem. Jewell was probably my oldest friend, and we were pleased that the men in our lives had bonded over their shared passion for fishing—an activity that seemed to be the male common denominator in these parts.

"About ten minutes more," said Jewel, when I came inside from the deck. The kitchen was bright and shiny, with stainless steel counters and lots of windows looking out onto the lake and trees.

"Great. That'll give us time to look at your latest pictures of Samantha."

Jewell had recently been to Ann Arbor to visit her daughter and new grandbaby, so I knew this would be a welcome subject. Soon I was admiring photos of a baby girl dressed in various ruffled outfits, smiling and drooling.

"Well, I never had kids, so I'll never be a grandmother." After the words slipped out, I was appalled that I couldn't just stay in admiration mode without bringing the conversation around to my sad childless self.

But Jewell didn't mind. "That's true," she said. "But remember, you've got Brooke. And when she has kids, I'm sure you will be an honorary grandmother."

"I hadn't thought of that. But who knows if that will ever happen? Right now she shows no signs of settling down."

"Hey, the girl just finished college. She needs to have some adventures. Give her time."

"As far as I can tell, she doesn't even have a serious boyfriend."

"In some ways, she's a lot like Derek," said Jewell.

"True. But tell me, what do you know about those two?"

"As far as their relationship?" She shook her head. "Tracy, it's all a big mystery to me. I know they always keep in touch. But when I inquire, Derek says he thinks a lot of Brooke and they'll always be good friends."

"I guess it's hard for me to grasp because I didn't have any guy friends like that when I was young. Did you?"

"Heavens, no. Guys were either boyfriends, potential boyfriends, or the boyfriends of my girlfriends—but things are so different now. They have coed dorms. Kids get jobs and room together."

"I suppose it's good, in a way."

"I think maybe it is. Nowadays the opposite sex doesn't have to be such a big mystery." The timer on the kitchen stove rang out, cutting short our ruminations about changing gender relationships. I went outside and walked down the wooden steps to call the men for dinner.

Shortly afterward, Frank was pouring the wine while Paul dished up the salad.

The meal was excellent. The salmon was fresh and Jewell had baked the filets with sour cream and slices of onion. As predicted, the wine was just right. The four of us were relaxed as we shared small talk about the current influx of tourists and part-time residents. Every summer the town's population more than tripled, which gave us all something to complain about, even while we knew that tourism was the lifeblood of the town.

But eventually the topic would come back to somebody's job. "How are things going at the hospital?" I said to Jewell.

"Some days everything is fine," she said with a sigh, "but lately there are days when I wish I was still a staff nurse and not having to make big decisions."

"Didn't I hear something about having to fire on of the nurses?" I said.

"Yes, you did—and the whole thing was painful. Registered nurses are hard to find, and I actually liked this woman, but she was stealing drugs."

"How did she manage that? Aren't all the drugs locked up?"

"This gal had a system," said Jewell. "She was on the surgical unit, usually carrying the keys to the drug cabinet. Then, when a patient asked for a pain shot, they only got half a dose and she injected herself with the other half."

"Oh, so the patient had to endure..."

"A lot of unnecessary pain. So she's gone." Jewell was clearly ready to change the subject. Turning to Frank, she said, "Speaking of high-stress jobs, what are you and Benny investigating these days?"

"Mainly the body on the beach."

"I understand you have it identified," said Paul.

Frank nodded as he reached for the cornbread. "We know who it is."

"A local?"

Frank shook his head. "From Big Rapids."

"What was he doing over here?"

"Not sure—but he might have been at a beach party."

"Is that where he went into the lake?" said Paul.

"Looks that way."

Paul topped up wine glasses, but when he came to Jewell, she waved him away, her expression serious. His wife was so quiet that he finally said, "Jewell, what's on your mind?"

Jewell took a deep breath and then said, "I was just thinking...didn't Derek go to some kind of beach party? And wasn't it about two weeks ago?"

"I don't even try to keep track of that boy," said Paul. "He's here for a night and then he's off to see his friends. He certainly doesn't check in with me."

I wondered if maybe Paul was trying to downplay his wife's suggestion—that Derek might have been at a party where somebody drowned. For a moment I debated on whether to add my own two cents. Finally I felt compelled. "Jewell may be right," I said. "I remember now—a while back I heard Brooke complaining to Derek that he went to a beach party without her because she had to work the late shift."

"I guess there could have been any number of parties on Lake Michigan that night," said Paul.

After a brief silence, Frank spoke up. "That's true," he said, "but just to be thorough, I'd better have a talk with Derek."

"In that case," said Paul, "you need to catch up with him soon. He's getting ready to fly back to Arizona."

I felt sorry for Frank as it became clear that his comment was casting a shadow on our pleasant summer evening. But before I had time to give the situation much thought, there was another development.

"Actually," said Jewell, "I think that's Derek's truck that just pulled in."

CHAPTER THIRTEEN

Detective Frank Kolowsky had a problem.

Here he was, an invited guest at the home of Paul and Jewell Lavallen. The dinner had been excellent, the conversation relaxing. But now he really needed to have an official talk with their son Derek, who had just informed them that he was holding a ticket for a 7:00 a.m. flight to Phoenix.

As Frank saw it, he could handle this in one of two ways. He could let Derek fly back to Arizona and plan to interview him by telephone—but he knew that a long-distance interview would be less than satisfactory. Or he could insist on talking to Derek that evening—in which case there was a good chance that Paul would be offended. Their relationship was now on friendly terms, but neither of them had forgotten their first contact when Paul himself had been a suspect in a murder investigation.

While Frank was mulling his options, Derek had joined the group and was sitting with them on the deck, laughing as he badgered his mother for a second piece of cheesecake.

Frank made his decision. "Derek," he said, "I'm really sorry to do this right now. But, with you leaving tomorrow, I need to ask some questions before you go." He glanced around at the group. "And it needs to be in private."

"Sure, no problem," said Derek, the only one who had no idea why he was suddenly so important.

"Well, then," Jewell said to her son, "why don't you and Frank go down to the dock and try out that new bench your father just built."

"Sure," said Derek, let's do that."

Frank avoided Paul's glance as he and Derek excused themselves and walked down the wooden steps to the boat landing. They stood for a moment and admired the sunset. Finally Frank spoke. "Guess you don't know what this is all about."

"Not a clue," Derek said with a grin.

"Okay," Frank said as he pulled the tiny spiral notebook from his shirt pocket and the two of them sat down. "What it's all about is that beach party you went to a couple of weeks ago. You see, it's possible that one of the guests at that party ended up drowning."

"Oh, like maybe—the guy that washed up on the beach?"

"Yep, that guy."

"Now I get it," said Derek. "What would you like to know?"

"Pretty much anything you can tell me about the party. But let's start with the location."

"It was at a summer place on Lake Michigan. I drove down Scenic Drive, but it wasn't easy to find, that's for sure."

"How did you hear about it?" said Frank.

"I saw a buddy in town that afternoon, and he told me about it."

"Did you go alone?"

"Yes, I did. I talked to Brooke, and it turned out that she was working. But I had nothing going on, so I picked up a six-pack and headed out."

"Tell me how you got there."

"I was trying to follow the directions this guy gave me, but of course I never wrote them down," said Derek. "I went south, but when I got to Stoney Lake, I knew I'd gone too far, so I turned around and drove back until I found a two-track leading into the woods."

"Which way?"

"Toward Lake Michigan. It was one of those private roads—you know, the kind that has a sign with the names of all the people who live back there."

"Like a private development," said Frank.

"Right. I think the whole thing was called DuneGrass. I had a house number, but none of the houses had numbers, so that didn't help. Finally I spotted a place with a lot of cars and figured that was it. Had to park along the road."

CHAPTER THIRTEEN

"So, how many people were there?" Frank said as he jotted notes. "What age?"

"I'd say most were college age—at least twenty people when I arrived—and more kept coming. Then somebody went down to the beach and built a bonfire, so there were a lot of people moving up and down the stairs."

"See anybody you knew?"

"I saw Bruce, the guy who invited me. And he introduced me to the host, whose name was Jeremy. I think most of the crowd was summer people. And then there were a couple of guys from Chicago who said they were working at that camp out there—the one with the funny name."

"Kobmoosa?"

"Yeah, that one."

"Okay. How did the evening go?"

"The usual stuff," said Derek. "Just drinking, hot dogs, and horsing around. I went down to the beach and mostly stayed there—helped gather driftwood for the fire. Sometimes a guy and girl would wander off down the beach and disappear for a while. You know how it is—once you're away from the campfire, there's no light at all."

"I get the picture. Was it just beer?"

"There was a bottle of Jack Daniels. But I missed out on that. Oh, and one girl brought a bowl of Jell-O shots."

"Those are interesting," said Frank. "They go down easy and pack a punch."

"That's for sure," said Derek. "At one point a couple of guys who had been taking Jell-O shots dared each other to go for a swim."

"So did they?"

"Yes, they did."

****

"Did you see that happen?" said Frank. He was suddenly glad that he had insisted on this last minute interview with Derek Lavallen. "Did you see the guys go into the water?"

"Yes I did," said Derek. "Like I said, Jell-O shots."

"And did they both come back out?" Frank had stopped scribbling in his notebook.

"Yes, they both came out."

"And did they claim their clothes?"

"They both came out and got dressed."

"You're sure about this?"

"Yes, I am. I remember because Jeremy was there, and he asked all of us to please not go in the lake anymore. "

"And nobody did?"

"Nope. Everybody settled down."

"Do you have a last name for Jeremy?"

"No, sorry." Derek shook his head. "He said the place belonged to his uncle. He was staying there for a few days and doing some chores for him."

"Okay." Frank scribbled silently for a moment before he continued. "Were there any arguments—any fights?"

"No, it was all pretty peaceful. Bruce, he's the one who invited me, Bruce said that two guys had got into it earlier, but the rest of the group talked them down and then they were best buds again."

"Anything else?"

Derek hesitated a bit before he said, "Well—there might have been some marijuana."

"I'm not the drug squad, Derek. So how late did the party last?"

"I think it was about midnight when things started to break up. Jeremy came down from the house and asked us to please keep the noise down."

"What caused that?"

"Not sure. Maybe a neighbor complained. So that kind of killed the mood."

"What time did you leave?"

"Shortly afterward. Got home sometime after one."

Frank jotted a few more notes. "Anything else I should know?"

Derek stood and looked out at the lake while a loon cried softly in the distance. Then he turned to Frank and said, "No, I can't think of anything else."

The two of them proceeded up the stairs but Frank paused at the landing and said, "I just remembered—the newspaper last week had a picture of our guy. Do you think your parents would have a copy of the paper?"

"Probably. They get it every week."

"Let's take a look at it. And you can tell me if you think you might have seen this guy at the party."

When they got back to the house, Jewell was making coffee. Paul located the latest issue of the *Shagoni River News*, which featured a photo of Tony Braxton on the front page.

"Did you see this guy at the party?" Frank said as he showed the photo to Derek. It was a high-school graduation photo provided by Tony's girlfriend, Brandi.

Derek spent a moment studying the headshot before he answered. "Nope. Didn't see anyone who looked like that."

"Okay," said Frank. "I guess that's all I need from you. Thanks for your time."

"No problem," said Derek. "Is it okay if I go now? Brooke is getting off work, and I want to see her before I leave."

"Just give me a phone number," Frank said, "so I can call you if I have any other questions."

After Derek told everyone good night and disappeared, Paul and Frank went to the garage to discuss the installation of new outriggers on his boat. Jewell laughed as she showed Tracy their new multifunction blender, an anniversary gift from their daughter.

"I'm not sure I'm mechanical enough to even use this," she said.

The mood was light as the four of them had coffee and said their goodnights. Nothing further was said about Derek or the beach party he had attended. Tracy and Frank were on their way home when he said, "I hope Paul wasn't upset about me collaring Derek the way I did."

"He was a little quiet while you two were gone," she said. "But I think he understood. How was your talk with Derek?"

"He answered all my questions. At first I thought I'd found the beach party where our victim went in. But then Derek couldn't match the photo in the paper to anyone there, so we just don't know. None of that was Derek's fault, though. It seemed like he was doing his best to be helpful."

"Derek's a good kid."

"Yes he is, but still..." Frank lapsed into silence.

"But what?"

"For some reason, Tracy—I have this gut feeling. I feel there's something Derek isn't telling me. Something important."

CHAPTER FOURTEEN

"Frank, I wish you weren't always thinking the worst of people—there's no reason Derek would lie to you."

"I didn't say he lied...maybe he just forgot to tell me something."

"It's a part of you I don't like. That you're always so suspicious of people."

"I'm that way because of my job, Tracy."

"Well maybe you should retire."

"It probably wouldn't change me any."

I couldn't come up with any good response, so I resigned myself to being silent for the remainder of the ride home. This was not the first time we had touched on the issue, and it never seemed to get resolved. Probably we'd make up when we got to my house—or not.

But just before we got into town, Frank did something that surprised me. "It's still early," he said. "How about we stop at the Brown Bear for a drink?"

"Okay," I said, mainly because I couldn't think of any reason to refuse.

The Brown Bear, a rustic bar featuring moose heads and deer antlers, was about half full when we arrived. The first people we saw were Joe and Annie Middlecamp, a retired couple from Detroit I had recently interviewed for the paper. They invited us to join them, and I was ready to accept but Frank refused, leading me to a corner booth that was pretty far away from the action. We had barely sat down when Frank asked me what I wanted to drink.

"Glass of wine, I guess."

"Okay, I'm going to the bar."

He returned shortly with my wine in one hand and a tumbler of golden-brown liquid in the other.

"Drinking scotch?" I said.

"Yep," was all he said, and he was barely in his seat before he chugged the whole thing down.

I was a little taken aback. In all of our time together I had never seen Frank consume alcohol with such urgency. Before I could register my surprise, Frank was back at the bar and returned minutes later with his second glass of scotch.

Clearly, something was going on. But what? Had I totally missed something that had upset him? Was it something that happened with Paul, or Derek—or did it have something to do with me?

That's it! This must be about me. Were we about to break up? How had I missed the signs? In over two years we had gone all the way from "friends with benefits" to "officially engaged" to "I'm not wearing your ring anymore because of that big kerfuffle over you spending the night at the home of your ex-wife."

And since then, perhaps, we had been limping along out of habit more than anything else, and I just hadn't noticed. How could I have been so blind??

I have never been good at talking about relationships. Certainly, I am incapable of having a civil conversation about ending a relationship. And right now it looked as though my soon-to-be-ex-lover was even more tongue-tied than me, since he was chugging down hard liquor to facilitate his exit. Finally, I couldn't handle it anymore. "Frank," I said, "talk to me."

He finished his second scotch, put down the glass, and looked across the table, barely meeting my eyes. His cheeks were flushed. "Okay then, Tracy—I need to tell you something."

Uh oh, here it comes. I bit my lip, determined not to cry.

"That is, I need to ask you something." Frank's face was so red that I wondered if he might be choking.

I was inclined to let him choke but realized I didn't want the local EMT's involved in whatever was coming next. "Okay," I said as calmly as possible. "Go ahead. I'm listening."

"I need a date."

He needed a date? Was he asking my permission to go out with someone other than me? Did it have to do with his job—like an investigation thing? Nothing was making sense. "I don't get this," I stammered.

"Let me try again. I'm inviting you—to—I'm inviting you—oh hell, are you free on the sixth of August?"

This was the big deal? We were *not* breaking up??

I took a deep breath and said, "Yes, I'm free as far as I know—need to check my calendar, of course. What's happening on the sixth?"

"It's, um—it's a wedding."

A wedding? So far, nothing explained all the drama we were enduring. But I had never been to a wedding with him; maybe he hated the whole concept. "Okay, fine," I said. "But who's getting married?"

"It's um—Jillian."

"Who—who's Jillian?" I knew I was sounding like an owl, and that I should know exactly who he was talking about. Actually, I did know. But the question came out anyway.

"Jillian is my ex-wife. She is getting married. And she wants me to be there."

"Frank, isn't that a bit crazy?"

"Yes, but no. But here's the thing—she is also inviting you."

For a moment I couldn't breathe. Finally I said, "That's crazier yet. I've never even met the woman."

"I told her I wouldn't go without you."

"Frank, that's the most ridiculous thing ever. I can't do this." I swallowed the last of my wine.

"Come on, Tracy, just think about it."

"I won't do it. I can't do it. You can't make me do it."

******

"Jewell, I can't believe Frank would ask me to do this."

"Tracy, he just doesn't want to be there without you. Isn't that sweet?"

"No, there is nothing sweet about it. The whole thing is perverted, as far as I'm concerned."

It was Saturday. I had pretty much shanghaied Jewell into meeting me in town, telling her I was in the grip of a mental health crisis that posed a danger to myself or others and quite possibly both. We were the only customers at the bakery, and I was working my way through a plate of lemon bars.

"I agree that it's a little unusual. Did he explain why Jillian wants him there?"

"It has something to do with the boys—the grandsons. They're going to be part of the wedding party—dressed up in tuxedoes."

"Aww, it sounds cute. But aren't they a little old to be ring bearers?"

"He made it sound like they're both going to walk with her down the aisle."

"Oh my goodness," she said. "Isn't it usually the father of the bride who does that?"

"I guess it used to be. Isn't that how you did it?" I said.

"Yes, as I recall."

"Well, not for me, with no father around. But my grandfather stepped in—as he usually did whenever I needed him. But doesn't this grandson thing strike you as a bit strange?"

Jewell smiled and patted my hand. "Tracy, this is the new millennium. Anything goes nowadays. Remember that wedding on the village green last summer where the guy had his dog as best man?"

"Sure, that was such a hoot that half the town came out to watch...not to mention a few stray dogs. We even put it in the paper."

"But think about this for a minute. It's good that Jillian is getting married, isn't it? I mean, from your point of view?"

"I don't see why I should care one way or another."

"Oh, come on. Weren't you bent out of shape about Frank staying overnight at her house?"

"Yeah, I guess—a little."

"So now she'll be married. No more opportunity for hanky-panky—imagined or otherwise."

"You might be right— yet again."

"Besides," Jewell said as she signaled to the waitress for more coffee, "remember when you mentioned that you were sad because you would never be a grandmother?"

"I never said that."

"Yes, you did. So here is your chance to acquire two grandsons."

"Oh lord. I was thinking more of babies...something a lot smaller than those two."

"See, you can just skip those formative years."

"Jewell, one of these boys is already a juvenile delinquent."

"Consider it a challenge. And there will be no diapers involved."

"But now maybe I don't want to be a grandmother."

"Tracy, I'm a grandma, and it doesn't hurt a bit. And face it, you are involved with a grandfather who wants you to be part of his life. His, ah, family life."

"But I just don't want to be at this wedding. Everybody will be looking at us...and wondering, *what are they doing here*?"

"Nobody will be looking at you. And if they do, they'll think that you and Frank make a striking couple. Who's she marrying, anyway?"

"Somebody named Curt." I bit into my third lemon bar. The sugar seemed to improve my mood. "Well, maybe," I said, "maybe I could do just the wedding and not the reception, if Frank will promise that we sit in the back."

"Okay, now we're talking. So what will you wear?"

"How about my long flowered skirt?" She shook her head. "My denim dress?"

"No on the skirt and double no on the dress. Absolutely not. How long has it been since you bought anything new?"

"I don't know. Maybe since I moved to Michigan."

At this point a tinkling noise emerged from Jewell's purse. She ignored the sound and said, "Tracy, it's true that you have nothing to wear—and that's why we need to go shopping."

"But there isn't a decent store within miles."

"I'll take you to Grand Rapids. We'll make it a day—go out for lunch."

"Hmm. Let me think about it."

"You'll need shoes too."

"I refuse to wear heels. They're awkward and make me feel like an Amazon."

"Stiletto heels are no longer in style."

"Good. Can I wear Birkenstocks?"

"Maybe. I understand they make some strappy sandals now."

At this point, the tinkling sound emerged from Jewel's purse again. "Sorry," she said, "I guess I'd better take this."

She fumbled for her purse and pulled out a cell phone. Her expression turned serious as she spoke and, after a brief exchange, ended the call.

"Tracy," she said, "I'm so sorry to bail on you, but I've got to go to the hospital."

"Right now?"

"Yes, I'm afraid so. That was the weekend supervisor, who has four people in the emergency room vomiting. Apparently there are more on the way—and the whole thing is beginning to look like some kind of food poisoning."

CHAPTER FIFTEEN

Jewell Lavallen found the hospital's emergency room parking lot filled with unauthorized vehicles. She parked on the grass and hurried inside.

Once through the glass doors, she felt like she had entered the first ring of Dante's Inferno. While she had done plenty of emergency room shifts in her career, and had coped with numerous hectic pileups, something made this scene unusual. Partly it was an indescribable odor that hung in the air like a miasma, but mostly, she decided, it was the noise level—the place echoed with retching and moaning.

She paused for a moment to figure out her next move. She glanced around and saw that every cubicle was occupied, and some were crammed with two patients instead of one. She peeked behind a curtain and saw one girl vomiting into an emesis basin and another girl getting an injection. Both of the patients looked quite young.

Jewell looked around until she spotted a tall man in blue scrubs, wearing rimless glasses and a harried expression. It was Don Fairchild, the nurse supervisor, holding two specimen jars while he struggled to write on a clipboard.

"Hey, Don," she said as she approached.

"Jewell," he replied, looking relieved, "thanks for coming in."

"No problem. What's going on?"

"Total zoo," he whispered.

"Who's on duty?"

"Dr. Nancy."

"Oh, this should be interesting."

Don managed a grin and said, "You got that right."

After two years at the hospital, Dr. Nancy Peterman had become a bit of a legend. She had begun her medical career with ten years in the navy and came away from that service with a vocabulary best described as salty. But her dedication and efficiency were beyond question.

"What was the ambulance?" Jewell said as she pulled a yellow gown from a shelf and shook it out.

"The ambulance was from a two-car crash on the freeway," Don replied. "Two people were okay, one was transferred out, and we kept one with a broken leg. Then a known cardiac with chest pain—we've got Jackie here doing EKGs. Then a kid who fell into the campfire and one impaled on a fishhook.

"But we were keeping up with all of that. I didn't call you until we got two carloads of teenagers all moaning and puking. At first Nancy thought it was some kind of mass hysteria. But now..." He paused long enough to sign a paper for an ambulance attendant. The phone on the desk started to ring.

"But now what?" Jewell tied the gown on over her clothes.

"This is no hysteria. These kids are puking their guts out—and some are bringing up blood."

"Sounds serious," she said. "Got specimens?"

"Right here." He held out the jars.

"I'll get them to the lab. Shall we call in another tech?"

"Trying to," he said. "Just paged Lily."

The phone rang and Jewell picked up. "Emergency room, may I help you?" To Don she whispered, "Anything else?"

"Yes, if you could." He pulled a ring of keys from his pocket and handed them over. "Get some IM Compazine from the pharmacy. We just used the last of our supply."

"Okay, I'm on it." And then, "Yes, Lily—we need you here—right away. Thanks."

During the next half hour, Jewell made trips to the lab and the pharmacy, restocked the med cupboard, and then stayed at the desk and answered the phone until one of the admitting clerks was able to take over. Then Jewell took the cardiac patient to a room and assisted with his admission. When she returned, the chaos in emergency room was decreasing.

She found Dr. Nancy at the desk looking over the intake sheets. The doctor, whose short hair boasted an unusual shade of red, wore a lab coat over black T-shirt and stretch pants.

"Hi, Nancy," said Jewell, "looks like you've been busy."

"Hey, Jewell," replied the doctor. "Yep, this place was busier than whorehouse with a destroyer in port."

"Looks like maybe things are getting calmed down," said Jewell. "Do you think it was some kind of bug?"

"Not sure," she said, "but lookie here." She pointed to the intake sheets. "Most, in fact all, of these pukes have listed their current address as Camp Kobmoosa. They're too young to be military—so where the hell is this camp?"

****

If Dr. Nancy had been a local she would have known about Camp Kobmoosa, maybe even have attended as a 4-H camper. But she was a newbie, a transplant from California who had somehow ended up as an emergency room physician in rural Michigan. Jewell proceeded to explain. "Kobmoosa is a summer camp for kids out by Stoney Lake. It's been there for years and has become sort of a local institution."

The doctor had no interest in the camp's reputation or longevity. "Okay," she said, "who brought these kids in?"

"Let's find out," said Jewell, who relayed the question to Don.

"He's right over there." Don pointed to a young man with curly hair who was leaning against a wall. "I think his name is Joel."

"We need to talk with him," said the doctor.

Jewell approached the young man and introduced herself. "I understand you brought these kids in from camp."

"Yes, I drove one of the vans," he said. "It was all pretty strange. Are the kids doing better?"

"Yes, they're doing better," said Jewell, "but the doctor wants to talk with you. Better come with me."

"Sure, no problem."

Minutes later Jewell convened a mini-conference in the doctors' break room. A small space, it offered standing room only to Dr. Nancy, Jewell, and Joel. The doctor got right to the point, addressing her questions to Joel. "So all of these kids are, ah, living out at this camp?"

"That's right." Joel nodded.

"And you live there too?"

"Been there since the first of May. Kids came in last week."

"What's your job?"

"Assistant to the manager. So I'm really a general gofer."

"Understood," she said. "Is there a camp doctor?"

"Not really. There's an old guy, Doc Brooty, who comes in and does physicals on the new arrivals, but he doesn't stay. The rest of the time, we have Lora—she's an EMT. Lora lives at the camp—runs the infirmary and handles first aid."

"Where is Lora now?"

"She just went downtown to get some gas. We each drove one of the vans from camp. She should be back any minute."

"Okay," said the doctor. "So nobody was sick until today?"

"Nope. Everybody seemed fine. Had their admission physicals and everything on Tuesday."

"Then this started—when? Today after lunch?"

"Yep. About half an hour after we ate." There was a knock on the door. Jewell opened it, and found Don there along with a thirtyish woman wearing jeans and a Camp Kobmoosa T-shirt.

"This is Lora," said Don. "She's the camp medical officer."

"Okay," said Dr. Nancy, "better bring her in too."

Jewell did quick introductions and said, "Now where were we?"

"Lunch," said the doctor. "I assume everybody ate in the mess hall. So how about you two?" She made a gesture that included Joel and Lora. "Didn't you guys get sick?"

"No," he replied, "Lora and I are still okay."

"And why do you think that was?"

"Well, the kids that got sick were all at the same table," said Lora.

"There are ten tables in the dining room," said Joel, "but neither of us sat at that table."

"And do you eat family style?" she said. "Does everyone at a table take food from the same serving bowl?"

"Yes. And I was thinking about that," said Lora. "The only girl who didn't get sick was the one who didn't like mac and cheese."

"It happened too fast to be any kind of bug," Dr. Nancy said with a glance at Jewell. "It's got to be food poisoning."

"I'm afraid you're right," Jewell replied, shaking her head as the implications became clear. "And you know what that means."

"It means we have to notify the goddamn health department," Dr. Nancy said with a grimace.

"Oh crap," said Joel. "Our boss won't be happy about this. Not one bit."

"Worse than unhappy," said Lora. "Dallas Bursley will go ballistic when she hears this."

"We'll have to flip a coin to see who gives her the bad news," said Joel.

"Enough about our problems," Lora said to the doctor. "What should we do about these kids?"

"We'll observe them for another hour," she replied. "If they're through puking, you can take them back. Make them rest and keep them on fluids 'til supper then a light diet for the rest of the day."

"We'll do that," said Lora. "Anything else?"

"Yes," said Nancy, "there is something else. Right now, one of you had better call the camp and get a message to the kitchen staff. Tell them to put the pan that held the mac and cheese into a plastic bag, label it clearly, and stick it in the refrigerator. Someone from the county health department will likely be out there tomorrow."

CHAPTER SIXTEEN

"Morning, Tracy," Brooke said as she came into the kitchen. I was eating a lunch of spinach and boiled egg in an attempt to cancel out my earlier indulgence in lemon bars during that interrupted heart-to-heart with Jewell.

"Hey, Brooke. I thought maybe you'd gone to work."

"No, just came back from Grand Rapids. Scott and I took Derek to the airport."

"So the fearsome threesome is no more."

"Right. Derek is on his way to Phoenix."

"Are you working second shift today?"

"Nope." Brooke got some ice water from the fridge and down across from me. "I actually have a Saturday off. Probably the only one all summer, so I'm going to enjoy it."

"Well, good. Got plans?"

"First of all a nap, then the beach. And tonight Scott is taking me to the casino for some kind of dinner theater."

"Sounds like fun. Are you hungry?"

"Nope, I'm good. We stopped for a burger on the way home."

"Okay, sounds like you'll be gone for dinner too."

"Right. And Tracy, how about you?"

"Frank's coming over."

"Well, great. You know I like Frank. Is everything good with you two?"

I generally tried to avoid discussing my love life with Brooke. But my talk with Jewell had been interrupted by her call from the hospital, which left me feeling...well, feeling like I still needed to talk to someone, even if it turned out to be Brooke.

"Oh, this will sound crazy."

"Crazy is fine with me."

"Well, here's the thing. Frank's ex-wife is getting married and..." I reached for the blue-cheese dressing and dumped it on my salad. So much for the calorie restriction.

"And what?"

"And he wants me to go to the wedding with him."

"That actually sounds like fun."

"Fun? I'd prefer a root canal. With no anesthesia."

"Fun," she repeated. "Especially If I can go shopping with you for the dress."

I stared at my young housemate, wondering if I had wandered into some hitherto-unknown realm where any problem can be solved by a shopping trip. That's when I realized that Brooke was still talking. "I think you would look really great in something asymmetric in a swirly pattern of teal blue and turquoise..."

So apparently I can avoid thinking about how awkward I might feel at the wedding if only I concentrate on what I am going to wear??

Finally, I stammered the only thing that came to my mind. "Umm, aren't teal and turquoise pretty much the same color?"

"Oh no, Tracy. Not by a long shot. Trust me, I took an art class."

That seemed to settle the issue for the moment. Brooke retreated to her room for a nap, and I didn't see her again for the rest of the day. She must have headed to the beach while I was at the post office getting mail.

It was getting on toward six o'clock when Frank showed up. We sat on the porch and watched the swallows that come out in the evening to swoop down for bugs. I mentioned that Derek was on his way to Arizona, and Frank said he really wished he could have had another talk with him about that beach party. I didn't want to stir up trouble, so I skated around the issue of Derek and pretty much tried to avoid our other burning question—the one about my attendance at Jillian's wedding.

But no such luck. "Have you thought any more about...August?"

"Well, yes. I told you I would think about it."

"Okay."

"And I still haven't decided for sure. But it seems like everything depends on—"

"On what?"

"On me finding the right dress to wear."

"Okay, then. That shouldn't be too hard." Frank stood and picked up the brown paper bag he had brought with him. "Guess maybe I should take this stuff inside."

He followed me into the kitchen, where he opened the refrigerator and made space for the bacon and maple syrup he took out of the bag.

"Looks like we might be having pancakes for breakfast," I said.

"Hope I'm not presuming too much." He turned and gave me a peck on the cheek.

"Like assuming that you will be invited to spend the night?"

"Yeah, like that."

"Let's just say the chances are pretty good—provided I get to choose tonight's movie."

We drove to Stanton for dinner and a movie and, on the way, engaged in the usual discussion as to which should come first. Since we were both hungry we decided to try a new Asian place where we shared several dishes with names like moo shu pork and kong min shrimp. It was all good. And so was the movie, which was the latest Star Wars offering—sequel or prequel, I forget which. When we got back to town, Frank did spend the night at my place. And that was pretty good too.

In the morning, he got up first and headed for the kitchen. By the time I got around to joining him, the place smelled of coffee and a short stack of pancakes was waiting for me.

"Oh, this is heaven," I said as I sat down and reached for the butter.

"No more than you deserve."

"You sure are in a good mood this morning."

"And rightly so. But do we have another taker for pancakes?" Frank was looking at Brooke, who had just come down the stairs in her pajamas.

"Oh, well—sure," she stammered. "I mean, it all smells so good."

"No problem," said Frank. "More pancakes coming up."

Brooke got a cup and poured herself some coffee. Then she got two plates and set them on the table. That's when I heard heavier steps coming down the stairs. "Another guest?" I said.

"Well, yeah," she replied with just a hint of hesitation. "If there's enough."

"Always plenty of pancakes," said Frank.

Seconds later a stocky guy with brushy blonde hair and a big smile appeared beside her.

"Hey," she said. "You guys remember Scott, don't you?"

****

"So, this guy Scott," said Frank. "Is he the new man in Brooke's life?"

"Looks that way," I replied.

"Did you know about this?"

"Not until this morning. I found out the same time you did—when he appeared for breakfast with us."

"But I thought that she and Derek..."

Frank and I were spending Sunday afternoon at his cabin on the Shagoni River, which runs through the Manistee National Forest. We were eating venison sausage sandwiches because Frank is a hunter who has a dozen ways to eat what he kills. Venison is an acquired taste, just like other aspects of being with Frank, but I'm making progress.

"Brooke and Derek are good friends," I said. "Then Scott appeared, and the three of them have been doing stuff together."

"Seems like Derek told me he was leaving yesterday morning," said Frank.

"Yes. They took him to the airport in Grand Rapids."

"And by evening this guy has made his move. I guess we could call him a fast worker. Were you surprised?"

"Yes and no. I guess I should have seen it coming."

"How so?"

"There was a little bit of chemistry between those two from the time they met."

"When did that happen?"

"It was at my house a couple of weeks ago. Brooke was cooking dinner, and Derek invited Scott over. After supper they all went off together. Then a day or two later—remember, you were with me at my place—Brooke and Scott showed up with all that fruit."

"Oh yeah, all those peaches and apricots."

"Right, and I was a little surprised that Derek wasn't with them. But most of the time they all did stuff together. I called them fearsome threesome."

"But now Derek is gone," he said.

"Yep, and this morning Scott crawls out of her bed. Oh dear, now I'm sounding judgmental."

"Yep, we're sounding like old farts."

"Guess it's really none of our business."

"None of our business," said Frank, "except that it's happening in your house. Do you feel okay about this guy?"

"Oh sure, Brooke has good judgment. Nothing wrong with Scott."

We finished our sandwiches and topped off the meal with sweet cherries. That was one reason I couldn't complain about Brooke seeing Scott—he kept us supplied with so much produce that I never knew what I was going to find in my refrigerator.

After lunch Frank and I took a hike along the river to work off our food. When we got back to his cabin it was after four o'clock. He brewed some coffee and, when we had finished it, I said, "It's time for me to be heading back to town."

"So soon?"

"Yep, that's why I have my own transportation."

"Well darn, foiled again."

I had brought my own car because, on previous Sundays, I had found that Frank would keep me at his place as long as possible. Although that was flattering, I discovered that it didn't give me enough time on Sunday evening to reset my brain to work mode..

So I got back into town around five, which I figured gave me plenty of time to do some chores, have a shower and then choose between TV and a mystery novel. There were a couple of messages on my answering machine but I ignored them, reasoning that none would be from Frank and there was no one else I wanted to talk to.

An hour later, I played the messages. One of them was a telemarketer and the other was from Ivy Martin.

"Tracy," she said. "I'm going to be in town, and it's really important that I see you. I have some big news."

Big news? She was using that ploy yet again? I considered my response. I had left Frank's house early so I could prepare for Monday, so it didn't make any sense to talk to Ivy and get drawn into whatever her current drama might be. And Ivy's life was almost always drama. Sometimes it concerned a boyfriend and other times it was her lack of a boyfriend. I had no intention of returning her call.

But then, just as I sank into my recliner and found my bookmark in the latest Sue Grafton mystery, a little silver car pulled into my driveway.

A car door slammed and I heard a voice. "Hey, Tracy, I'm here."

Ivy Martin bounded onto my porch and was through the screen door before I could consider a response. Certainly hiding was not an option.

"Oh, hi," I mumbled.

Now she was in my living room. "Hey, girl, it's been so long since I've seen you that a person might think you've actually been avoiding me. Haha. So here I am, and I intend to drag you down to the Belly Up for a drink—and boy, am I ready for a pizza."

"Oh, Ivy, I don't know."

She ignored my response and continued. "Hey, did I tell you that I heard from Steve? But so far I haven't replied...not sure I want to go there again. Are you in touch with him at all?"

"No, not a word."

The aforementioned Steve was my ex-husband, who had been in town about a year before, when he had gotten involved with Ivy, which had led to him drinking too much, which had led to him being belligerent at a party, which had led to him spending a night in the local slammer.

"It was just an email," she said. "Guess I won't respond. I've got other fish to fry right now. Hey, get yourself together and let's hit the bar."

"I don't think so. I was planning to wash my hair tonight." Even to me, my excuse sounded feeble.

"Not a chance, Trace." She sat in my grandma's favorite chair, the one with all the crocheted doilies. "I'm not leaving here without you."

Based on previous experience, I knew that my choices were limited. If I wanted Ivy out of my house, the easiest way to make that happen was to go with her.

"So, tell me," I said, "what is your big news?"

"I won't tell unless you come with me."

She was dangling the bait again. Sometimes nothing but a cheap trick, but sometimes it did pan out. Besides, I was a little bit hungry. My resistance was starting to crumble. "Ivy, you go ahead. I'll meet you there."

"No way. Come on, ride with me. I'm not poison."

I had to smile at that because Marge often referred to her as Poison Ivy. I think it's because Ivy used to work for Marge and they parted under less than ideal circumstances.

The upshot was that I put on clean jeans, ran a brush through my hair, and climbed into the little silver car next to Ivy, reasoning that I could walk the five blocks home if I really needed to get away before she did.

The Belly Up Bar was about half full when we arrived, the clientele divided among locals that I knew, tourists that I didn't know, and summer people who looked vaguely familiar because I might have interviewed them at one time. We made a beeline for the only available booth, where we settled in and ordered beer and pizza.

After the beer arrived, I said, "So, what's your news?"

"It's about that guy on the beach."

"You mean the dead one?"

"Of course the dead one." Ivy pulled a compact from her purse, checked her reflection, and powdered her nose. "Word is that he was involved in some kind of love triangle."

Where does she get this stuff? Is she making it all up?

"So the other guy killed him?"

"Maybe."

"So what is your source?"

"Strictly confidential. Hey, excuse me, I'll be right back."

Ivy disappeared down the hallway that led to the restrooms. She was still gone when the pizza arrived, so I waited about a minute and then decided to go ahead. I picked up a slice and struggled to detach the strings of cheese before I took a bite.

When I looked up, I saw Ivy standing at the bar talking to a guy I didn't recognize. This was not unusual. Ivy was very good at initiating small talk with strangers, especially if the strangers were men between the ages of twenty and eighty. Seconds later she touched him on the shoulder, then turned and rejoined me.

"Take a look," she said as she sat down and addressed herself to the food. "See the cute guy at the bar?"

"Yes, I noticed. Is he an old friend?"

"More like a new friend," she said with a giggle. "But he seemed nice. So I hope you don't mind, but I asked him to join us."

CHAPTER SEVENTEEN

The guy approaching our table was somewhere between attractive and ordinary—about six feet tall, sporting khaki pants and a blue polo shirt. His moustache was neatly trimmed, but his hair was thin on top and arranged in a rather desperate combover. His blue eyes sparkled behind wire-rimmed glasses as he approached our table, and the smile he flashed looked almost genuine.

"Good evening, ladies," he said. "I'm here all alone and would be thrilled to have someone to talk to."

As a pick-up line it was not exactly original, but it was better than some I'd heard. Ivy was busy wrestling with a slice of pizza but, when she looked at me for confirmation, I gave her a half-hearted shrug. "We'll give you a try," she said, "but you'd better behave yourself." She scooted over to make room for him. "Tracy, this is Mark."

He sat down and reached across the table in an effort to shake my hand. "Mark Antonelli. I'm from Chicago."

I waved away the handshake, indicating that my fingers were covered with cheese. "I'm Tracy," I said. "And I live here."

"Well, aren't you lucky the lucky one. This place is paradise."

"Try us in January," I said, providing my standard answer to summer visitors.

Ivy took a sip of her beer and said, "Mark was just telling me about the Chicago- to-Mackinac sailboat race."

"I've heard about it," I said. "I used to live near Chicago. When does the race happen?"

"The race is pretty much winding down right now," he replied. "The boats left Navy Pier Saturday—there are over three hundred of them, so they don't leave all at once. Start times are staggered throughout the day. They should all be at the island by now."

"Sounds like a big deal," said Ivy.

"It is," he replied. "And actually, it's the reason I'm here. Because after the race, most of the boats take their time going back to Chicago, and a bunch of them are planning to stop overnight in your little town. So next Saturday your yacht club is hosting a dinner event, calling it the Back-from-the-Mack Party."

"Oh that," I said. I vaguely recalled Marge telling me I should cover the event.

"What's your connection?" said Ivy.

"My uncle Jack is one of the racers, and he'll be stopping here on his way back to Chicago. Dad has a cottage on Lake Michigan, so I'm spending a few days with him—and I'm in town today to get tickets for the yacht club event."

"Sounds interesting." I felt myself slipping into reporter mode. "I'm with the local newspaper. Maybe I can interview your uncle. What's the name of his boat?"

"It's the *Northern Star*," he said. "And they expect to be here on Wednesday or Thursday."

"Can you put me in touch?" I said.

Mark pulled a card from his wallet and pushed it across the table to me. "Call me in a few days, and I'll see what I can set up for you. His name is Jack Bloomgarden. And I think you'll enjoy meeting him. Jack is a big talker, and his favorite subject is his boat."

"Hey, don't forget me," said Ivy. "I'm a writer too."

Mark pulled out another card and slipped it to her. "Ivy," he said, "you can call me any time."

I stayed at the bar awhile longer, long enough to eat another slice of pizza and finish my beer. When I announced my intention to walk home, both Mark and Ivy offered to drive me, but neither of them looked crestfallen when I insisted that the walk would do me good.

"I plan to be in touch with you," I said to Mark as I slipped his card into my pocket. "And hopefully I can talk with your uncle who owns the *Northern Star*. It sounds like a good story."

"I'm happy to be your contact," he said. "Jack likes his beer, so you can probably meet with him right here."

"Sounds good." I had cleaned the grease off my fingers, so this time I shook his hand.

"Tracy, aren't you glad you came out with me tonight?" said Ivy. "I said you would never learn anything sitting at home."

"Oh Ivy, I just hate it when you are right." We both had a chuckle.

And once again I found myself thinking—well, damn, sometimes it pays to hang out with Ivy Martin after all. If I had to cover the yacht-club party, I liked the idea of meeting with Captain Jack first so we could have a private talk, which would be less hectic than trying to converse during the actual dinner party.

So I was feeling pretty positive during my walk home—although, before I arrived, I found myself wishing I had worn a jacket. There were a few spatters of rain, the wind had come up, and it felt as though the temperature had dropped ten degrees.

It was still daylight when I got home. I took Mark's card from my pocket and put it on my desk, noticing that he listed both a cell phone and a business number and the card said he was in real estate.

So my time with Ivy had been useful after all. And what was that other bit about the dead guy on the beach? A love triangle? Just gossip, but something to mention to Frank when I saw him again.

****

On Monday it was obvious that our summer heat wave had been displaced. The wind was blowing, and rain showers were coming and going. I welcomed the change in the weather and arrived at work in pretty good spirits. Marge was in her office, wearing a purple dress that was definitely not her color. I said good morning, and asked if she still wanted me to cover the event at the yacht club for the sailboats returning from the race.

"Of course," she said with a sigh that suggested that I was both forgetful and incompetent. "Didn't you write it on your schedule when I told you last week?"

"Just checking. Also, could I maybe do a feature story on one of the boats? I've got a chance to talk to one of the captains when he comes in this week. That would be Jack—ah, Jack Bloomgarden of the *Northern Star*."

"Guess that would be okay," she said. "Just don't make it too long."

"They tell me he's a talker."

"Sailors usually are."

"You can always shorten it," I said. "That's the nice thing about features."

"Okay," she said, "and don't forget the zoning board this afternoon. I think Sadie Berkowitz is on the warpath."

"Poor Sadie. What's her problem?"

"You know she had that hobby shop downtown."

"I remember. What happened to it?"

"What happened was that she razed the building with plans to replace it with a four-unit condo—and now the board says they won't allow it. She's fuming."

"Guess she didn't see that coming."

"She should have checked it out first," said Marge, "but anyway, that's it for now. And do close my door on your way out."

One thing about my boss—you know when you've been dismissed. So I spent most of the afternoon with the zoning board where I endured long-winded discussions about the unwelcome profusion of condos downtown, and exactly how tall a three-story building could be. I got some indignant quotes from Sadie, which perked up my story but probably wouldn't change the board's decision.

Brooke was working, so I was happy to spend a quiet evening at alone. I thought about calling Frank but never got around to it so I went to bed early—well before Brooke got home. The rain was coming down steadily, and I let the sound lull me to sleep.

But I didn't get to sleep through the night.

I was awakened by a crack of thunder so sharp it might have been gunfire. Checking my clock, I saw that it was 3:40 a.m. I crawled out of bed in time to see a bolt of lightning light up the room and then heard an eerie, high-pitched moan that I couldn't identify. I fumbled with the bedside lamp and, when it didn't respond, I realized that the power was out.

I wondered if the rest of the village had power, so I pulled aside a curtain to check the streetlights. But I didn't see any. In fact, I couldn't see anything at all. As I stared into the utter darkness, there was another loud *crack.* I thought it was thunder, but it seemed to go on too long. A knock on my bedroom door made me jump.

"Is that you, Brooke?"

"Yes, it's me. Are you okay?"

"I'm okay. Come on in."

The door opened, and I could just make out a figure holding a flashlight. "Tracy, what was that noise?"

"Guess we're having a storm."

"Is there anything we should do?"

Her face looked eerie in the yellow glow of the flashlight. "Let's see if the phone is working," I said.

Brooke did her best to light the way as we stumbled into the living room and I picked up the receiver, thinking that I would call Frank. But there was no dial tone. Clearly I didn't need Frank to tell me there was nothing we could do—except wait for daylight.

"Nothing we can do until morning," I said. "We might as well try to get some sleep."

I stumbled back to my bedroom, grabbing furniture along the way. Brooke followed me and paused at the door. "I was wondering," she said.

"Yes?"

"I was wondering if maybe I could, um, share your bed?"

CHAPTER EIGHTEEN

The next morning Brooke and I had a cold breakfast. There was no rain, the sky was beginning to clear and the wind had settled down. I offered to drive her to work but, once we got outside, I had to retract my offer. A big chunk of tree had come down and landed in the driveway effectively blocking in my Honda.

"Guess I won't be driving anywhere today," I said.

"No problem," Brooke replied cheerfully. "I usually walk anyway."

My housemate said good bye and set off. I lingered long enough to do a cursory inspection of my car which revealed a dented fender and a lot of scratches but nothing that appeared to be serious. I tugged at the limbs that were pinning it in place and discovered they were far too heavy for me to budge.

So I grabbed my purse and walked four blocks to the office, where I found the lights off but the door unlocked. Marge was inside, and so was my fellow reporter Jake Billington. We soon established that the entire village was in the dark.

"Not much we can do without power," I said.

"That's not true," said Marge. "Jake's been here awhile, and he's been through this before. So Jake, tell her what we do."

"What we do," said Jake, "is you sharpen your pencil, take your steno pad, walk downtown and talk to people. Everyone will have a story to tell."

"That's what we'll do," said Marge. "We should divide this up. One of you go downtown, and one of you head to the marina and the beach. Jake, which do you want?"

"I'll take the waterfront," he said.

"Okay. And you, Tracy, head downtown."

So I walked to the town's business section, where I found shop owners out on the sidewalks, most of them commiserating about their experiences during the night. The consensus was that nobody in town had been injured and nobody in town had power.

I approached Jim and Ellie Nordstrom, who owned the ice-cream shop, and asked them how long their product would last without refrigeration. "At least forty-eight hours," Jim said, "and longer if we take the right measures. It depends a little on the weather."

"So what measures do you take?" I said, as I pulled out my steno pad.

"First of all, we keep the place closed up," said Ellie.

"And we put insulating blankets over the freezers," said Jim. "So we could probably last a third day, but that would be pushing it."

"And then what would happen?"

"What would happen is, we start giving away free melting ice cream."

The next person I interviewed was Todd Melrose, who owned a restaurant that was famous for hamburgers. "My problem," he said, "is all that frozen meat. Once it thaws out, it has to be used. I can't refreeze it. The health department has some very strict rules."

"So what is your emergency plan?" I said.

"If we don't get power by sometime tomorrow, I'll haul out a grill and start cooking burgers for city crew, and for anyone else in town."

"That should make you popular."

"It's a small town," he said. "Good will is worth a lot."

Just then we were interrupted by a high pitched whine. "What on earth is that?" I said.

"That is the blessed sound of a chain saw."

I had never before considered that sound a blessing, but under the circumstances, I was inclined to agree. I followed the sound and arrived in front of village hall, where folks who would usually be sitting at desks were out in the street. The village manager, Neil Franklin, was looking good in a denim shirt and jeans as he worked with a volunteer crew dragging limbs out of Hancock

Street.

"I see the press is here," Neil said when he saw me.

"Yep, just trying not to get in the way."

"Oh, you're never in my way," Neil said with a smile. "And look who's here." He waved to a tall man in blue coveralls. It was Lyle Makin, the public works superintendent.

"How are things in the rest of town?" I said.

"We don't know yet, but we're planning to find out," said Jim. "Lyle here is just about to do a survey."

"Hey, could I ride shotgun with you?" I said to Lyle.

"No problem," he said. "Hop on board."

Lyle tossed a chain saw into the bed of a red pick-up while I climbed into the passenger seat. Our trip around town brought frequent encounters with downed trees in the streets, which necessitated detours and occasional U-turns. Residents were in their yards, surveying damage and gathering brush. If they waved at him, Lyle would stop for a moment to talk, and everyone wanted to know about getting power. They all got the same answer, because nobody could say for sure when electricity would be back on. Almost the entire county had been affected.

As he traveled, Lyle occasionally turned on a crackling two-way radio, which he used to report the most serious road problems. At one point he got out of his truck and cut some branches off a fallen tree to clear his own way. "This may not be a top priority," I said, "but my car is trapped behind a tree."

"Is it on a public road?"

"Nope, it's in my driveway."

"Sorry," he said, "but it's not a priority."

"That's kind of what I thought."

"Holy cow, look at this one," Lyle said as we approached the sprawling Maclarn house, reputed to be the oldest in the village. It dated back to the days when lumber barons had made their fortunes by sending timber to Chicago.

The house had tall elm trees in the yard, and one of them had split in two, with half of the tree landing on the house. That half had smashed the stone chimney and broken clean through the roof of the living room. The owners, an elderly couple, were in the yard taking pictures of the damage. Lyle stopped and spoke with them, determined that nobody was hurt, and said he hoped their insurance was current.

Eventually he headed for the waterfront. As we approached, I spotted a small group of people gathered on the breakwater between the channel and the yacht club. One member of that group looked a lot like Frank Kolowsky.

"Hey," I said to Lyle, "could you let me off here?

CHAPTER NINETEEN

When I climbed out of the DPW truck, Frank spotted me and started walking in my direction.

"Hey, Tracy," he said.

"Hey yourself," I said as he and favored me with a one-armed hug. We had developed some pretty strict rules about public displays of affection after a couple of embarrassing incidents early in our relationship.

"What are you up to?"

"Been riding around with Lyle while he surveyed the streets. How about you?"

"I came into town because I had a call from Ron, the marina manager. He said a couple of boat owners were complaining that their dinghies had been stolen."

Marina manager Ron Raulins, a burly guy with reddish hair, was standing next to Frank, and he spoke up. "I wouldn't have bothered you, but they were pretty darned upset."

"As it turned out," said Frank, "the dinghies had come loose during the storm. We found them on the other side of the lake."

"I think I'm going to offer a class in knot tying," said Ron.

"So then Ron and I went to check the campground and the state park," said Frank. "There was a trailer that had blown over, so we helped get them back on their wheels."

"Did you see Brooke?"

"Yep. She was there with a posse of kids who were collecting lawn chairs and other stuff that had blown around, and returning it all to the rightful owners."

"I do believe she has a future working with young people."

"How's things at your house?" said Frank.

"Not too bad," I said. "Except I can't get my car out because a limb came down in the driveway. Guess I'll need the services of your trusty chain saw."

"I'll get at it today."

"Thanks. What about your place?"

"No damage at all. You know my house is surrounded by pine trees. They break the wind a little, and they're not tall enough to get blown over. My driveway is a different matter—I had to cut my way through it."

That's when I realized that the group of people standing at the seawall was growing. Chief of Police Jerry Lauter was there, as well as June Florinda, current commodore of the yacht club. "What's everybody doing here?" I said to Frank.

"I believe we're waiting for a couple of sailboats to show up."

"Sailboats? Something to do with the race?"

"Well, yes."

"But we had that huge storm last night. Were they out in that?"

Frank heaved a sigh before he answered. "I guess it's no secret, so I'll tell you what I know. But none of this is for the paper—okay?"

"Sure," I said as we stepped away from the group.

"As I understand it, there were several sailboats that left Mackinaw yesterday heading for Chicago. They got word of the storm, and most of them decided to take refuge, either in Traverse City or Manistee. But at least one of them took a gamble and stayed on the lake, planning to reach here before dark. However, they lost the gamble. The boat overturned and they lost one of their crew."

"Lost...as in, they can't find him?"

"No, Tracy. Lost as in dead."

"Oh...how sad."

We were quiet for a few minutes. Everybody else was quiet too, looking down the channel, speaking very little. The sky was overcast, suiting the mood.

Finally I said, "Do you know the name of the sailboat that, ah, lost a crew member?"

"I don't know," said Frank, "but somebody here will." He approached June, the yacht club commodore, and said, "Do you know the name of the sailboat?"

"I do," June said, "just let me think for a minute. It was something to do with a star...yes, it was the *Northern Star*."

The *Northern Star*—that was the boat Mark had been talking about, the one that belonged to his uncle from Chicago. And one of their crew was dead. I leaned against Frank while we waited. About ten minutes later someone announced, "There they are."

Along with everyone else, I stared down the channel toward Lake Michigan. Finally I saw what our sharp-eyed lookout had spotted.

Two boats were motoring down the channel, heading for the dock where the sad little reception committee was waiting.

****

STORM TURNS DEADLY ON BIG LAKE; LAKE MICHIGAN CLAIMS ANOTHER LIFE; FIRST EVER FATALITY IN RACE HISTORY.

As a rule I do not write headlines for the paper. I submit the stories and then Marge comes up with a headline that will suit the paper, both graphically and content wise. But today was different.

After the better part of two days without power, we were now in emergency mode. For the front page, we had to determine which was the bigger story—the power outage in the village or the death on Lake Michigan. Marge, Jake, and I were in a huddle trying to decide.

I made a suggestion. "It seems to me that the stories are both storm related. So how about one big headline about the storm...and then two subheadlines, one about the village and one about the—the sailboat."

"That just might work," said Marge.

"Okay," I said. "I've got things to do."

And one of those things was to call Mark Antonelli and see if his uncle Jack would be willing to talk with me. I fully expected the answer would be no, but when Mark got back to me, I was surprised. "Jack said he would meet with you," said Mark. "I guess it's something for him to do other than sitting around thinking."

"That's great," I said. "How about tomorrow morning at the yacht club?"

"We can do that," he said. "I'll drive him into town. Considering the state he's in, we don't want him driving anywhere on his own."

By the time I arrived at the yacht club the following morning, Commodore June already knew what I was there for, and thoughtfully offered to let me use her office for the interview. She ushered me in and told me to go ahead and use her desk. The room had one small window, and the walls were covered with marine charts and photos of boats and lighthouses.

Minutes later June brought in Jack Bloomgarden and introduced us. The man looked to be somewhere in his sixties, with a face that might have been handsome but for the purple bruise around his left eye and several scratches, which could have been from the accident or from a recent shaving mishap.

"I'll get you two some coffee," said June.

"That would be wonderful," I said.

Once the coffee arrived, I poured two cups and saw Jack struggle to control his shaking hands while he reached for his. "Thanks for coming in," I said. "I know this must be very difficult for you."

That was all it took to get him started.

"The whole goddam thing was my fault," he said. "Absolutely. Completely. I'm the captain, for god's sake. And I knew the storm was coming, but we all talked it over, all five of us, and figured we could make it. The boat is a catamaran, and they're hard to tip over. I've been through some bad weather in that boat before. With most of the same crew. I guess that's why we were so damn confident.

"So we stayed out. We were about three miles offshore when everything went to hell. It was blowing and raining like hell, but we thought we had it under control. Had the sails down, of course. But then something happened—we're still not sure what. Near as we can tell, we got sideways of a huge wave, at the same time that a blast of wind came up and knocked us over. I was at the helm, but whatever I did must have been wrong. In any case, we went over. At first I couldn't believe it was happening...the deck went vertical, and I slid over the rail and into the water.

"As soon as I surfaced, I started doing a head count. Pretty soon we had everybody accounted for except Doug. When we were on deck, everyone had their tethers fastened...you know what that is...keeps you tied to the boat. But once we went over, I unhooked my tether and so did everyone else. Everyone except Doug. We think the boom hit him on the head and he wasn't conscious to unhook himself. So instead of saving his life, the damn rope kept him underwater while he drowned.

"Just before we capsized, we had put out a distress call, so before long a couple of boats came out to help. They took us on board, notified the coast guard, and one of their guys went down to try and find Bruce. By then it was dark, and he had no luck. Finally the coast guard arrived and their diver went down, found Doug, and brought him out. Of course it was too late. He'd been dead for over an hour."

I didn't understand all of the nautical terms Jack was using, but I didn't ask any questions. I figured the best thing I could do was to let him continue until he ran out of steam.

CHAPTER TWENTY

My interview with Jack Bloomgarden, owner and skipper of the ill-fated *Northern Star*, went on for almost two hours, and there was very little I could do other than listen. I had no platitudes to offer.

Jack said it over and over, that he held himself responsible for the death of his crew member, twenty five-year-old Douglas Freeborn.

"His family is devastated. I know they will never truly forgive me."

Eventually, I realized that listening to him was the only thing I could do and, in a sense, it was the best thing I could do. By now he had reviewed every step of the tragedy multiple times. He had spoken with the sailors who rescued him, the coast guard, his family, Doug's family, and the local marine officer; he had told the story again and again.

And while I was never a psych major, I sensed that each retelling somehow relieved a minute amount of the terrible pressure Jack was carrying. He was right in believing that this was something that would never be over, but putting the events into words perhaps gave him a tiny sense of control.

It was almost noon when he finally ran out of words. I wrapped up our conversation with a few innocuous questions about the history of the race. "Thanks for talking with me," I said as we stood and shook hands. "Mark said you're staying with his dad out at the lake."

"Yes, but I'm heading back to Chicago this afternoon."

"How about we have some lunch before you go?" I remembered that Mark had said his uncle was drinking more than eating since the tragedy. In any case he responded to my suggestion.

"Might be a good idea," he said. "I didn't have any breakfast."

We both ordered sandwiches and sat on the deck to eat them. Fortunately, there were no other guests around, so he didn't have to deal with questions or even glances from strangers who might have recognized him. "So, you won't be here for the party on Saturday," I said.

"No. I want to get back to Chicago and see what I can do for Doug's family. My god, they're making funeral arrangements for their only son. No one should have to do that."

"Did you know them well?"

He shook his head. "I knew Doug because he went to college with my grandson. We had him at the house for a couple of holidays."

"You never met his parents?"

"No, but I will now. The whole thing is ironic because he loved sailing so much and I felt like I was doing him a favor when I took him out with us. He did the race with me last year, and we all had a great time—but now this."

For a while we sat in silence, taking in the view. Shagoni Lake was calm, with just enough breeze to move a pair of sailboats, one of them boasting bright red sails.

"Think you'll continue sailing?" I said.

"Not sure." He took a drink of his iced tea. "Want to buy a sailboat?"

****

Back at work, I wrote up my interview with Jack, then finished another story and had a brief meeting with Jake. It was well after six when I finally left the office. On my way out I met Holly coming in with cub reporter Kyle. They appeared to be in high spirits, both giggling about something. "Hi, you two," I said. "How's it going?"

"Good," Holly said. "We just came from the that new llama farm, and I got some great photos."

"She got spit on, but only once," Kyle said with a grin.

"Also, I wanted to tell you, Tracy—about a piece of news I picked up. It's about Camp Kobmoosa."

"Were you out there?"

"No," she said, "but I did see Joel yesterday—remember Joel?"

"Sure. The guy who worked out there."

"Joel had the afternoon off, so he came into town. We rented motor scooters and took a ride up to Bass Lake."

"Sounds like fun. What was the news?"

"There was a big hassle at camp a couple of days ago. A whole bunch of kids got sick and started puking. They took them to the ER, and most of them got shots and everybody got better. Then, a couple of days later, the health department came around asking questions."

"I'll bet the boss didn't like that," I said, thinking of Dallas Bursley and her worries about bad publicity.

"You're right. He said what's her name—Bursley—has been in a bad mood ever since."

"Poor Joel. No wonder he wanted to get away for an afternoon."

So now there had been incident at Camp Kobmoosa. And it made me wonder again—was someone trying to sabotage the place? And if so, why?

****

WELCOME BACK FROM THE MAC.

Despite the cheery welcome sign and the crowd of people at the yacht club Saturday night, the atmosphere was somewhat subdued—which was only to be expected. The news of the death of a crew member on the *Northern Star* was like a fog that hung over the entire event.

I walked through the main hall, where the band was playing and a few couples were doing a respectable rendition of the Charleston. Next came a smaller room where I found my way to a table and met two men, both from the Chicago area, who were owners of sailboats in the race. I explained that I wrote for the local paper, and they were happy to tell me about their boats, their crew, and their love of sailing.

Still, like a needle swinging to magnetic north, the conversation came back to unanswered questions about the death of the crew member on the *Northern Star*.

"Shouldn't have happened."

"First death ever—poor judgment?"

"Maybe just bad luck."

"Don't understand it."

"Do you think Jack had been drinking?"

That's when I put away my steno pad and just listened to their conversation. More people joined the group, which grew to include crew members of other boats, some of them from the rescue boat—and every one of them wanted to review the tragedy yet again.

I understood their position, but felt that I had heard more than enough of the sad story. I excused myself, walked away and looked around for somewhere else to be. So I was actually happy to see Ivy when she appeared. Ivy was all decked out in a white blouse with a pattern of nautical flags, and (believe it or not) lighthouse earrings that flashed on and off.

"Hi, Tracy," she said when she saw me. "I'm here with Mark, and we've got a table. Want to join us?"

"Sure. Sounds good." As I followed her back to the main room, I tried to figure out who this latest guy might be. Within seconds, I remembered that Mark was the one who had put me in touch with Jack Bloomgarden, who was what—maybe his uncle? I had all of this figured out by the time we reached a round table in a corner not far from the bar. Mark was sitting with a silver-haired man who looked like an older version of himself.

Mark greeted me and said, "Tracy, this is my dad, George Antonelli."

George shook my hand and said, "Nice to meet you, Tracy—and let me get you a drink. What's your poison?"

"Gin and tonic," I blurted, before I remembered that I had a strict policy of buying my own drinks.

"Coming up," he said as he headed for the bar.

George Antonelli returned shortly, bringing not only my drink but also a generous plate of smoked oysters and shrimp. "Hey, this looks good," said Ivy as she reached for an oyster. "You must have some pull around here."

"Not exactly pull," said George. "I stole it from a waitress who was balancing four plates. I told her she needed to get rid of one before she dropped it."

At that point the band took a break and a guy in a suit took the microphone. He welcomed everybody and introduced a woman who made a speech about something and then she introduced another guy who made a speech about something else. I paid limited attention to the speakers because the four of us were quietly sharing jokes and muted conversation.

We were having a pretty good time, and it made me remember why I put up with Ivy, despite her sometimes irritating habits. Though none of us got boisterous, our silly jokes seemed to get more and more hilarious. Maybe we all just needed a break from whatever serious things were weighing us down. I never knew who it was, but somebody flipped an ice cube in my direction and it landed in my lap. I grabbed it and threw it back. Eventually it landed on the floor, and we were debating whether it was okay to leave it there or whether it posed a safety hazard. Like a good citizen, I left my chair and bent down to retrieve the ice.

When I looked up, I saw Frank Kolowski standing in the foyer. He looked around as though he were casing the joint, and that's when I remembered that we had talked about meeting at the club if he was in town. Frank saw me and his rugged face broke into a smile. I stood and flagged him over to our table.

"Hey, Tracy, good to see you."

"Glad you could make it," I said and proceeded with introductions. "You know my friend Ivy, of course."

"Of course," said Frank. "Everybody knows Ivy."

"And the ones who don't certainly want to," she simpered.

"This is Mark," I said, "and his father, George. Meet my friend Frank Kolowsky."

Mark nodded and said, "Hello, nice to meet you."

But George stood so he could shake hands with Frank. As he did so, he said, "I believe we have already met."

"I believe you are right," said Frank.

"You are the detective."

CHAPTER TWENTY-ONE

While Frank was at the bar getting a drink, Ivy procured another chair and placed it between hers and mine. When Frank returned, she made a point of passing him the seafood plate.

"Only two oysters left," she said. "We saved them for you."

"Thanks."

"And you know what they do for your love life," she said with a wink. "If you two need any help, just call me." Frank made no response, so she tried a new tack. "I think somebody is stalking me," she said. "I probably need the services of a private detective."

"Call the office Monday," he said. "Sheriff Benny will be glad to hear your complaint."

I had heard this banter before so did not find it upsetting. Still, it was a relief when the band started up, which caused Ivy to turn her attention to Mark and maneuver him onto the dance floor. That left the three of us at the table. George Antonelli and Frank had no trouble engaging in conversation about some manly topic, probably either cars or fishing. I didn't listen much to what they were saying, but I was happy to feel Frank's considerable bulk parked next to me.

Mark and Ivy returned to our table, finished their drinks and chatted a little longer before they excused themselves and headed out. Mark's dad followed their lead. Then, not much later, Frank and I decided to leave. Our departure took about twenty minutes, since each of us got stopped in turn by somebody with a burning question.

Finally we made our escape. Frank followed me to my house, where we parked our vehicles in the driveway he had recently cleared. Once inside, we decided that we didn't need any more alcohol but agreed that ice cream was definitely in order.

We found some rocky road, a jar of chocolate sauce and a tin of walnuts. We filled our bowls and, minutes later, were in my living room, hunkered down on the sofa with our dishes on the coffee table. "So, tell me," I said, "how did you know George Antonelli?"

"I might ask you the same thing," he replied. "He seemed to be plying you with drinks."

"Oh cripe, that was just an accident." Frank seemed to be waiting for a further explanation so I said, "He caught me off guard in the beginning and then, every time my glass was even half empty, another one appeared. Hey, you're not jealous are you?"

"Don't have the energy for that," he said, planting a kiss on my cheek. "Jealousy is a young man's game."

"Well, good. I noticed you two seemed to recognize one another. Is there some history I don't know about?"

"Yes, but it's nothing personal. He's got a place on Lake Michigan, and he's the one who called us when he found a body on the beach."

"Oh, that body—"

"Yep, that one."

"Any progress on whodunit?"

Frank was quiet for a moment while he attended to his ice cream. "To be honest, not much, beyond identifying the young man. But his parents are back in the country, so I'm going out Monday to talk with them."

"Hey, isn't Antonelli's place pretty close to Camp Kobmoosa?"

"Yep, just a mile or so down the beach."

"I heard there was an incident out there—food poisoning or something."

"You heard right. The health department reported it to us, so now I'm obliged to pay them a visit. How did you hear about it?"

"I got this from Holly, our summer intern. She has a friend at camp named Joel."

"At first it sounded like bored kids trying for some excitement. But then

Dr. Nancy mentioned the possibility of arsenic. So it definitely needs to be looked into."

"Frank, do you think there's any connection here?"

"Connection? How?"

"Between the body on the beach and the problems at camp?"

"Other than sharing a shoreline, I don't see any. What are you thinking?"

"Remember, I said that Mort Fitzgerald, the county commissioner, mentioned an out-of-town group wanting to do a lakefront development. And they were hoping to buy some land from the camp."

"Yeah, I guess."

"Well, it would be to their advantage if Kobmoosa had problems...and needed money."

"If I follow your thinking, you're saying that sabotage might be in order."

"Right."

"Well, maybe the arsenic thing, but I really don't think they would turn to murder."

"I guess that would be pretty drastic."

We focused on the ice cream until our attention was diverted by the sound of a vehicle in the driveway. That was followed by car doors slamming, laughter, and footsteps on the porch. Seconds later Brooke came through the door carrying a paper bag.

"Hey, guys," she said when she saw us. "Did you leave me any ice cream?"

"I think so," I said. "Just look in the freezer."

"Great. And Frank, I've got something to tell you."

Brooke disappeared into the kitchen. Minutes later she returned holding half a cantaloupe filled with ice cream.

"Hey, clever bowl," said Frank.

"It looks like you just spent some time with Scott," I said.

"You guessed right." Brooke sat down and dug into her treat.

"Hey," said Frank, "you said you have something to tell me."

"Oh that." She paused to lick her spoon. "Well, you know Derek and I keep in touch. Yesterday we talked and, Frank, he wants you to call him. Said he remembered something."

"I'll do that," Frank said. "Did he give you any idea what it was about?"

"It was about that beach party. He said something about chex mix. Not sure what that means. Have you ever heard of chex mix?"

"No, but I guess I'll find out," said Frank. "I'll call him tomorrow."

CHAPTER TWENTY-TWO

"I can't believe that Tony was engaged. He never mentioned anything about a girl."

"It's impossible. The boy didn't even have a job."

Frank was talking to Gordon and Joanne Braxton, parents of Tony Braxton, the young man whose body had washed up on the beach in Cedar County.

Frank made notes as they talked. He also observed. And everything about these people screamed normal, middle class, and strictly law abiding. Both parents were teachers; he taught high school history, and she taught middle school English. The house was ranch style, the cars were midpriced, the lawn was mowed. And of course, these two were struggling to deal with the death of their only son.

After an hour, Frank had not unearthed anything except an average American family with an average American boy who played basketball in high school, enjoyed camping, and was good at fixing cars. In college, Tony had changed his major a few times, finally ending up with a degree in economics. Neither Tony nor his parents had ever had a prescription for Flexeril.

That's how things stood when the sister arrived. Her name was Zoe, her hair was blue, and she had just finished her first year at Michigan State. When she joined the conversation, the news she brought knocked her parents off balance.

"Oh my god, Mom, you mean you never met Brandi? They were all over each other—and yes, he even bought her a ring."

"How in hell did he buy a ring?" said her father. "He never had any money."

"I think he got a credit card," said Zoe.

"A credit card? But how?"

"Oh, Dad, in college you get all kinds of applications in the mail."

"We never should have gone on our trip," said her mom.

"I don't see how that could have made any difference—he never listened to us anyway."

Tony's mom wiped her bloodshot eyes. "We thought maybe there was a girl, but we didn't know who it was. After the holidays, we hardly ever saw him."

"Sure, Mom, and that's why," said Zoe. "He spent every waking hour with this girl and, believe me, they had wedding plans."

"Are you sure?"

"Sure I'm sure. I saw them over spring break, and Brandi asked me to be a bridesmaid. She couldn't wait to be Brandi Braxton."

"What on earth was he thinking?" said her father. "No money, no job, no place to live."

"According to Brandi," said Zoe, "they had that all figured out."

"What do you mean?"

"What they told me," said Zoe, "was that Brandi's dad owned a car dealership in Wexford. Tony was going to work at the dealership, and her dad also owned an apartment building. They could live there and be the managers."

Gordon shook his head. "I still can't believe it."

Frank cleared his throat. "Not to interrupt on a family matter," he said, "but it looks like your daughter is at least partially right."

"What do you mean?"

"When we found your son's body, there was no identification on him. So we looked at missing person reports—and we found one. It was out of Big Rapids, submitted by a young woman named Brandi Fairchild."

"That's her," said Zoe.

"She identified herself as his fiancée. Said they had been living together."

"Oh lord," said Gordon. "We thought he was living with two other guys."

"And Brandi is the one," said Frank, "who drove to the morgue and identified the body."

"So now you know," said Zoe. When her parents were silent, she added, "I think the two of you should talk to Brandi."

"What on earth for?" said the mom.

Zoe moved to the sofa, sat next to her mother and took her hand. "Look, Mom, we have to plan a funeral—and I think that Brandi needs to be involved."

"I don't see why."

"Because she was in love with Tony, that's why. She was a big part of his life."

"She'll come to the funeral anyway," said the dad.

"Can't we have a something private? Just the family?"

"Mom, Tony was young. He had tons and tons of friends."

Frank cleared his throat. "This sounds like something you need to discuss as a family."

"We'll do that," said Zoe.

"But while I'm here, can you think of anyone who had a grudge against Tony?"

Dad said no. Mom shook her head.

"Zoe, you're closer to his age, might know his friends. Can you think of anyone?"

After a moment's silence she said, "No, I can't."

"Guess that's it for now," Frank said as he stood to go. "Thanks for seeing me, and I'm certainly sorry for your loss."

Zoe stood and said, "I have a question for you, detective."

"I'll answer if I can."

"Okay." She took a deep breath. "All we know is that he was found dead on the beach and the, ah, postmortem said that he drowned."

"That's right. There was water in his lungs."

"And this was the morning after some kind of beach party."

"Yes, although the body washed up some distance from the site of the party. We still haven't found anyone who can place him at the party."

"Here's the thing we're still not clear on," said Zoe. "Was it an accident?"

"Maybe," said Frank, speaking slowly as he chose his words. "But in a case like this there are three possibilities. One is accidental death and another is suicide—did he ever seem depressed?"

"Never," said Zoe. "He was in madly in love—everybody could see that."

"And then," said Frank, "we have to consider murder."

"Murder?" she said, her voice getting shrill. "Why would anyone want to kill my brother?"

"That's what we're trying to find out."

****

"I been cooking for thirty-eight years and never had anything like this before. I just hope it don't go on my record."

"I guess that will be up to your boss," said Frank.

Teresa Matulis, the cook at Camp Kobmoosa, was a solidly built woman. She wore an industrial-sized apron over denim overalls and a red bandana around her head. "Oh yeah, Ms. Bursley. See, I been here eight years, and I been through three different directors. I just wish they would leave me alone to do my job. I don't see why they have to keep changing menu. Kids are too picky these days. If they're hungry, they eat...that's what my mother always said. She was from the old country—came over by ship and was so sick the whole time she would never go near any kind of boat the rest of her life. She always..."

Frank realized that the woman would keep talking until she was interrupted. So he said, "Did you save the baking pan that had the mac and cheese for table number ten?"

"Yes, it's all in plastic bags in the fridge. Bottom shelf. Actually, there's two pans in there because by the time I got the word, we weren't for sure which one it was, and one of them had been put to soak. They all look alike, you know."

"Okay," said Frank. "Now, would you show me how you make the mac and cheese?"

"Sure," she said. "First we boil the pasta—in this a pot." She indicated a five-gallon stainless steel container on the stove. "When it cools down a little, pasta goes into these tins." She indicated a dozen tins about the size of bread pans.

"Do you do all of this yourself?"

"Yep. Then I make a sauce." She showed Frank a five-pound bag of yellow powder. "I mix this with milk, then pour it over the pasta, and put slices of cheese on top. Then we bake it."

"Okay. Who works with the food other than you?"

"Well, there's my assistant Bonnie—and always one of the kids, one of the campers on KP duty."

"Can you tell me the name of the camper who was working that day...it would be last week Saturday?"

"Sure, let me look at calendar." Teresa spent a few minutes looking through drawers before she replied. "Sorry, can't find it right now."

"Well, maybe you can find out and let me know."

"Sure. I'll tell Ms. Bursley and have her call you." She glanced at the clock above the stove.

"And then one more question. Do you keep any rat poison around?"

"Well, no—not this time of year."

"Meaning?"

"We put some out in the fall when we close up."

"And then what happens to it?"

"When we clean in the spring, we throw the rat poison in the trash."

Their conversation was interrupted by a girl in shorts and pigtails who appeared in the doorway. "Do you want me to start setting the tables for lunch?" she said.

"Have you filled the water pitchers?" said Teresa.

"Oops, I forgot."

"Pitchers come first," she said. "Look at your list."

"But I lost my list."

"Then look at the bulletin board." Teresa shook her head and said to Frank, "Kids. You got any?"

"Oh yeah," he replied. "Boy and a girl. Marbles for brains at that age. I wouldn't want your job."

"I wouldn't want yours either," she said smiling for the first time, which revealed a gold tooth.

"Anyway, thanks for your time," Frank said. "I know you must be busy feeding all these kids—and try to find that name for me, okay?"

"I will. And I tell you one thing. I'm pretty sure it was one of the boys."

Back in town, Frank dropped a clunky package on the sheriff's desk.

"What is this?" said Sheriff Benny.

"Baking pans from the kitchen at Camp Kobmoosa."

"And what are we supposed to do with them?"

"Send them to the lab to be tested for arsenic."

"We can do that," said Benny, "but you know how long that lab takes. Summer camp could be over by then."

"I know," said Frank, "but what else can we do? It's not like anybody died."

"So, let me get this straight. The health department called us because a bunch of kids at camp got sick and they all wound up in the emergency room."

"Right."

"And they all recovered."

"They did. But Dr. Nancy Peterman was in the ER that day and she didn't think it was food poisoning. She's the one who suggested checking for arsenic."

"So that's why we need to send off these smelly bags full of dirty dishes?"

"Right."

"Okay. Want to grab some lunch?"

"Sure. Let's go."

Frank and Benny walked to the Pink Elephant, where they both ordered the roast beef special. The place was busy, but the staff prioritized their orders and the food arrived promptly.

"Did you talk to anyone else at camp today?" said Benny.

"Yep. Started with Dallas Bursley, the director. And of course she was horrified about the incident. I understand that she was hired to turn things around and attract new campers."

"Arsenic in the lunch not be a big selling point."

"Right. People are so fussy these days." Frank finished his coffee. "What have you got on for this afternoon?"

"Just paperwork. How about you?"

"I need to interview someone out on Lake Michigan. Care to come along?"

"Sure. You'd probably get lost without me."

CHAPTER TWENTY-THREE

"His name is Max Merrifield," said Frank, "and he lives near Reed City, if I remember correctly."

"That's a fair distance," said Sheriff Benny. "How did he end up owning a cottage on Lake Michigan?"

"I guess that's one of the things we'll find out today."

The two of them were in Frank's car, looking for a subdivision on Lake Michigan called DuneGrass. Frank turned off the paved road onto a two-track that snaked over a dune and then dipped into a grove of pine trees. "Damn," said Benny, "I've lived in Cedar County all my life, and these roads still get me all mixed up."

"Probably this road wasn't here fifty years ago."

"You may be right. Back then it was all beach."

"Did you come out here for beach parties?"

"Hell, no. I was a farm boy—had to swim in the river."

"Lucky you," said Frank. "I learned to swim in the YMCA pool."

After a few more turns and a rickety bridge, the men located the cottage they were looking for and Max Merrifield stepped outside to greet them. Merrifield, a thin man in his forties, wore khaki pants and a button-down shirt. He invited them in and led them through the house to a deck with old-fashioned wicker furniture. "Have a seat," he said. "Can I get you some coffee?"

"Coffee would be good," said Benny as he eased his weight into a fragile-looking chair.

Merrifield disappeared for a moment, leaving his guests to admire the view of Lake Michigan. "That looks like an ore carrier out there," said Frank.

"Long and skinny," said Benny, "like the *Edmund Fitzgerald.*"

"Probably heading to Chicago."

"Hope you don't mind instant coffee," said their host as he came out bearing a tray with three mugs. "I don't spend much time here, so it's a bit like camping out."

"Instant is fine," said Frank. "How long have you owned this place?"

"Just over a year," said Merrifield. "It belonged to my great uncle, who died a couple of years ago without a will. So last summer the probate court notified me that I was the legal heir—and also that back taxes were due. Big surprise. I had only been here a couple of times when I was a kid."

"It's a nice place," said Benny.

"Yes, it is," said Merrifield. "Would you like to buy it?"

"Are you serious?"

"Maybe, maybe not. My wife and I were shocked by the tax bill. It's a burden for us, so we talk about putting it up for sale. But the neighbors assure us that we could rent it out for a few weeks in the summer and make enough to cover the taxes."

"Plenty of people do that," said Benny.

"Right," said Merrifield, as he took a seat. "But I guess you didn't come here to talk real estate."

"That's right," said Frank. "We need to know about your nephew, the one who was here over the July Fourth holiday."

"That would be Jeremy. He had some time off, so I gave him the keys to the place. The deal was that he was going to replace some boards on the porch and the deck."

"Did he do that?"

"Yes, and he did a good job. He's a better carpenter than I am."

"Good for him," Frank said as he pulled out his tiny spiral notebook. "What's his full name?"

"Jeremy Merrifield. My brother, his dad, is deceased."

"Where does Jeremy live?"

"Near Mount Pleasant. I try to see him every couple of weeks."

"Did you tell him he could have a party here?"

Merrifield took a sip of coffee. "Here's how I remember it. When we talked about him staying here, he asked would it be okay to have some friends over for a bonfire on the beach—and I said yes, as long as he cleaned up afterward."

"And did he?"

"Yes, he did. But from what I hear, the party got pretty big. People he invited brought people he didn't know, so it was more than just a few friends. But whatever went on, they took their trash out. I found a couple of stray beer cans, but other than that, the place was in good shape."

"That's good to know," Frank said as he scribbled.

"So, what happened, exactly? I mean, why are you here?"

"We're not sure what happened," said Frank. "You may have heard that we found the body of a young man on the beach about a quarter of a mile from here."

"I heard some stories, but they were all pretty vague. Do you think it was somebody from the party?"

"It looks that way—but so far, we haven't found anyone who can say for sure. So it would be a big help if we could talk to your nephew. Can you give us his phone number?"

Merrifield gave Frank a number and said, "It's a landline. He's living with his mother and taking classes at Central. Has a couple of jobs too."

"Sounds like an enterprising young man."

"He's doing okay. Jeremy did have a few bad years after his father died. He's not in any trouble, is he?"

"No trouble," said Frank. "We just need to find out more about the party. Do you think he'll be visiting again?"

"He might, but I don't know when. He stays pretty busy."

"I'll give him a call," said Frank.

"I'm glad to help. Want to walk down to the beach and have a look around?"

"Sure," said Frank, "just give me a minute. Okay if I use your bathroom?"

"No problem," said Merrifield as he stood and opened a door. "Just follow that hallway and it's on your right."

Minutes later the three of them made their way down a long flight of wooden stairs. Near the base of the staircase Merrifield showed them a circle of stones that had been used as a fire ring. Inside the ring was a pile of cinder and ashes with a few bits of tinfoil.

Frank kicked the ashes and said, "Well, you're right about them being neat. They didn't leave much in the way of trash for us to inspect."

****

"Did you find anything in there?" Sheriff Benny asked Frank as the two of them headed back to town.

"In where?' said Frank.

"In the bathroom," said Benny. "I know that trick. Just ask to use the bathroom and you get to do a mini-search without a warrant or even asking permission."

"Okay. I'll admit that I did peek in the medicine cabinet, and I found—well, nothing but a bottle of Tylenol, a tin of aspirin and some old toothpaste."

"So there was nothing prescription?"

"No, nothing like Flexeril or even Sudafed," said Frank as he navigated a turn. "Those kids really cleaned up after themselves. So maybe that's a clue."

"Meaning what?" said Benny.

"Meaning that most young men are such slobs, then if someone is neat, they must be covering up a crime."

"It's a theory, but not a great one," said the sheriff. "I read your report on the victim's parents. I don't see anything there that could help us."

"I agree," said Frank. "Every thing seemed pretty normal—except that Tony never told them about the engagement."

"Guess it happened while they were on that trip to Australia."

"The sister was obviously closer to him. I wonder if she could tell us anything."

"If you talk to her," said Benny, "check out a rumor. I heard that the dead guy was involved in some kind of love triangle."

"A love triangle," Frank repeated. "And where did you get this astounding clue?"

"I'm pretty sure it was from that girl reporter, Ivy Martin."

"I remember now—I saw her in your office the other day."

"Yep, she brought me some brownies."

"And you didn't save me any."

"Nope."

"Well, we both know that Ivy does like to wheedle information from people—stuff that's supposed to be confidential but sometimes ends up in her newspaper."

"You could say that," said the sheriff, "but I don't think we should go there. You have your own issues with female reporters."

"I guess you're right," said Frank. "But tell me about this love triangle thing."

"Well, that about covers it, don't it? It would mean there was another guy involved."

"Or another girl."

"It all seems pretty far-fetched," said Benny. "We need another theory."

"Okay," said Frank, "try this one. Maybe someone is trying to sabotage the camp down there."

"Sabotage? What do you mean?"

"First of all, the body was found pretty close to camp property. And then, about a week later, they had that arsenic scare."

"I see what you're getting at," said Benny. "But why would anyone have it in for the camp?"

"Real estate, that's why. I believe there are some Chicago developers who would love to build condos on that property."

"So now we're dealing with the Chicago mafia? How did you come up with this theory?"

"Let me think," said Frank as they neared the courthouse. "Okay, Tracy was at some event at the camp —and while she was there, she had a talk with the township supervisor."

"That would be Mort Fitzimmons."

"Right," said Frank as he pulled into the parking lot. "And I believe the camp sabotage theory came from Tracy."

"So there we go," said Benny as he unbuckled his seat belt. "Let's just sit back and let the girl reporters solve this case."

CHAPTER TWENTY-FOUR

"Morning, Tracy," Brooke said as she stumbled into the kitchen and poured herself a cup of coffee. "Do you want a refill?"

"Nope, I'm good, thanks."

"Those muffins look delicious."

"Yep. I'm on my second one. Try the blueberry."

It was Saturday morning, and Brooke and I were sharing a leisurely breakfast. For me, it was a day off and, for her, it was a late shift at work.

"I was wondering," said Brooke, "did Frank ever get in touch with Derek?"

"I don't think so. The last time Frank mentioned Derek, he said they hadn't connected." I reached for the plum jam. "Did he say what it was he wanted to talk to Frank about?"

"No, but I think I have a pretty good idea. Remember just before Derek left for Arizona, Frank talked to him about that beach party he went to?"

"Yes, I remember. Frank and I had supper at the Lavallens and Derek was getting packed to catch his plane."

"My guess is that it has something to do with that party he went to."

"Okay, I'll mention it again when I see Frank."

"And are you gonna see him tonight? After all, it is Saturday—or are you two...?"

Once again Brooke was taking a little too much interest in my personal life, so I changed the subject. "I didn't wake up when you came home last night. What were you up to?"

"I was out with Scott. He took me to something called a demolition derby."

"You make it sound like a public hanging."

"It was just about that entertaining."

"So tell me about it."

"Oh lord. Rednecks sitting on bleachers—I mean, bald guys with scruffy beards and fat women falling out of their tank tops. Beat-up cars crashing into each other. Noise and dust and gas fumes and people getting all excited about—I don't know what they were so excited about."

"You have my sympathy," I said. "I went to one of those on assignment, but I didn't have to stay very long."

"I told Scott I could never go back—it's bad for my allergies."

"Anyway, it looks like you and Scott are, shall we say, an item."

"I guess you could say that—but we both know it's just a summer thing. I'm looking at jobs right now, and the most promising ones are either Montana or Colorado."

"Oh, Brooke, they're both so far away. I'm going to miss you next summer." That's when I heard a knock on the front door. "Hey, I think we have company."

"That'll be Scott. He said he might stop by." She yelled out, "Come on in. We're in the kitchen."

The screen door slammed and there were footsteps down the hallway. When Scott reached the kitchen, Brooke stood and greeted him with a hug. I think he wanted to hug me too, but I stayed in my chair, so he had to make do with an awkward pat on my shoulder.

She poured him a cup of coffee and Scott sat down with us. Brooke talked about her latest work crisis when a toddler had wandered off and put the whole park on alert. Scott told a story about the time he rescued Jojo, the family pet, when that dog managed to fall through the ice during a fishing trip. Scott illustrated his stories with facial expressions, and his puppy-dog eyes made Jojo highly believable.

"After that, Jojo would never go fishing with us again," Scott said, as Brooke refilled his cup. "The poor dog was so traumatized she didn't even want to go outside in the winter."

At this point Brooke and I both had dog stories to tell.

Then Scott repeated the litany I heard every time he visited. "You know,

Tracy, I love this old house, and someday I want to have one just like it. I love the tall windows and all the woodwork and stuff."

"You probably wouldn't love it so much if you had to maintain it."

"I'm just waiting for my chance to mow your lawn," he said.

"Sure," I said with a laugh. "Maybe next week."

The lawnmower bit had been a standing offer ever since Scott started seeing Brooke, but he was never around when I really need him, and besides, I sort of enjoyed doing the job myself. Scott finished his coffee and said he had some errands to do before he headed to the beach. Brooke promised to meet him there around noon. After he left, Brooke took the bag of plums he had brought and stuck them in the refrigerator.

"Once again, we have bounty from the fruit stand," I said. "Scott is coming in pretty handy this summer."

"He's okay," she said. "But sometimes..." She trailed off as she stared out the kitchen window.

"Sometimes, what?"

"Sometimes he tells lies—about stupid stuff."

"Like what?"

"Well, for one thing, he said he played basketball in college—made a big deal out of it. But then yesterday he said not really, he wasn't on the team. He meant they just played pick-up in the parking lot. I'm not a sports nut, so I don't care one way or the other. But why do guys tell lies that make no sense?"

"Probably he's trying to impress you."

"Because he's insecure?"

"Something like that," I said.

"Oh god, who knows, but anyway—it's just a summer thing. I'm going to go take a shower—but don't forget to remind Frank about calling Derek."

****

Brooke headed off to work and I was alone until Frank arrived to take me to dinner in Manistee. We had decided to try a restaurant that Paul and Jewell had recommended. The place was busy when we arrived but we managed to score the last table on the deck. I decided on the fish special and Frank ordered a steak. We had both neglected to eat lunch, so we wasted no time when the food arrived.

"How's the perch?" he said.

"Pretty good. Kind of fishy, but that's what the lemon is for. And your steak?"

"It's fine. Maybe not quite as rare I would like."

"Oh, I know. You like it bloody."

"But I'm not complaining. I'm glad we came here."

"Me too. It feels good to get out of town."

The restaurant was called 440 WEST and it was on the river. Our location on the deck afforded a view of the river and even a peek at the drawbridge. "Got a question for you," he said. "Have you ever heard of something called chex mix?"

"Chex mix? Isn't that what people serve at bridge parties?"

"Not in this case, it isn't."

"So tell me."

Frank took some time to spread sour cream on his potato before he answered. "It's a term I just learned from Derek."

"So you finally had a talk with Derek?"

"Yes, I did. And he said there was something about that beach party that he forgot to mention."

"He forgot to mention chex mix? "

He paused for a bit of steak before he continued. "I guess it's a thing that teens do at parties. Before they leave home, they go into the parents' medicine chest. They grab anything that looks interesting—pain meds, antidepressants, uppers, downers, stuff with funny labels. When they get to the party, there's a bowl on a table and they dump in their offering. When the contents look interesting, someone stirs them up and kids will grab a handful and swallow them."

"Oh lord," I said. "And they probably wash it all down with alcohol."

"That would be my guess."

"And here I thought I'd heard everything. You know, I worked for that hospital in Illinois, and of course we had kids come into the ER with overdoses.

But this is something new."

"I guess every generation tries to outdo their parents in terms of craziness."

"Did Derek take any of this stuff?"

"Guess not. He told me he saw the bowl on the table and didn't even know what it was. Later on, down at the beach, a few guys were acting weird and someone explained they were enjoying the effects of the chex mix."

"Do you suppose that's where the dead guy got the Flexeril that showed up in his bloodstream?"

"Seems the most likely explanation."

"And since Flexeril relaxes muscles— "

"It would greatly interfere with his ability to swim."

"Oh, that poor guy." I imagined for a moment how he must have felt struggling in the water.

"But anyway," said Frank, "I think we promised each other not to talk business tonight."

"Yes, we did—neither yours nor mine. Time to change the subject."

But maybe it would have been better if we had continued to talk about chex mix and the dead body. Because Frank moved on to a subject I was not quite ready to discuss. "Look, Tracy," he said, "I really need to give Jillian an answer about the wedding. Have you reached a decision?"

"Well, yes, I have— "

But I stopped midsentence when a petite waitress with olive skin appeared at our table. Stammering a little, she asked if there was any chance that a couple who had just arrived could be seated with us.

"I'm so sorry to impose," she said, "but we are full up, and these two say they are friends of yours—good friends, is what she said. Of course, if you say no, I'm sure they will understand."

"What the hell?" said Frank.

Frank and I looked at each other and then peered through the glass doors into the darkened interior, where I spotted a dark-haired woman waving frantically at us.

"Oh my god," Frank whispered, "it's Ivy."

"Ivy and Mark," I said, noting the man beside her.

"Isn't this why we got out of town?"

"Guess it didn't work. What should we do?" I said.

"I guess it would be rude to say no."

"We are nearly done. We can always make up an excuse to leave. "

"Sure," Frank said, "invite them to join us."

"Okay." I signaled to the waitress.

"You never know," said Frank. "Maybe Mark can tell us something about the Chicago mafia."

CHAPTER TWENTY-FIVE

"What a stroke of luck," said Ivy as she raised her glass for a group toast.

"Mmm, so it was," I said, as I half-heartedly raised my half-empty wine glass, all the while wondering if Ivy would get through the meal without getting food on her slinky white tank top.

"Mark and I were just headed for the casino—still are, in fact—when I decided that I wanted the casino experience but not the casino food—you know what that's like, don't you? Overpriced and undercooked. So then I thought of this place and asked Mark if he was willing to give it a try. He said yes, and here we are. I told him this would be as good as any restaurant in Chicago. And it is—right?" Mark didn't reply so she prompted him. "Isn't it darling?"

"Yes, so far everything is good."

"But the place was full, and we really didn't want to wait. And that's when I just happened to see the two of you. So here we are, the four of us together again. Now, that's what I call luck."

Frank and I didn't talk much because we didn't need to. We listened to our tablemates—mostly Ivy —as we finished our entrées and selected dessert. I was making very little effort to follow the conversation.

But then Frank decided to partake.

"So, Mark," he said, "what is it you do down there in Chicago?" It was possible that Frank was being polite, or maybe he was really interested. But I suspected that he was slipping into detective mode.

"I've got my finger in a lot of pies," said Mark. "My dad and I bought up some vacant buildings in the city, and we'd like to upgrade them into apartments. You'd think it would be easy, because everybody is crying for housing, but it isn't. There's all kind of zoning regulations, building permits, red tape, and politics holding us up. Right now he's got some rental properties and other business concerns that I manage for him."

Then Frank brought the conversation closer to home. I thought he made the shift rather deftly. "What about waterfront property up in this area?" he said. "What future do you see with that?" Now Frank was sounding a bit like an entrepreneur himself.

"Dad is very fond of his beach house," said Mark, "and I am too, so that will stay as it is. As far as other developments on the lake, we've certainly talked about it—but it would require more money than we have. So that would mean finding investors and forming a corporation, which would mean dealing with lawyers and accountants. The whole thing would get really complicated."

"I've been to your father's place," said Frank, "and it's a great location. I understand there is some history involved."

"You mean the prohibition era."

"Yes, that. Supposedly, it was used as a drop-off for bootleggers."

"We've heard that story too. There's a little window on the third floor, and apparently a light in the window was a signal—meaning all clear, bring in the booze boat."

"Sounds like it might be a good feature story," I said.

"Please don't," Mark said quickly. "Dad doesn't need any more attention right now."

"Oh sure," I replied. "I wasn't thinking. It must have been a shock for him to find a body on his beach."

"It bothered him a lot," said Mark. "And shortly afterward, we were hit with Uncle Jack and his crisis."

"This is good, isn't it, darling?" Ivy said to Mark, who was well into his prime rib.

"Mmm, yes, very good."

"Told you so." Ivy drank some more wine. "Hey, Tracy, are you going to cover that music festival in August?"

"Music festival?"

"Down by Roxbury. It's a really big deal."

"Probably not. I'm hoping Kyle will want to do it. From what I hear, it's a young crowd that parties all night, and the bands are people that I've never heard of."

"Tracy, you sound like a senior citizen."

"I'm getting there."

"Well, I am definitely planning to go. I've got a press pass, of course, and I'm trying to get a ticket for Mark. We might even camp overnight."

At this point Mark weighed in. "Ivy," he said, "I'm not even sure that I can be here that weekend. I do have business in Chicago."

"Oh, poof, you can be here if you want to." She reached out and mussed his hair.

By this time, Frank and I had finished everything—our wine, our dessert, and coffee. I figured he probably wanted to escape, so I looked at my watch and said, "Well, guys, Frank and I are on a bit of a schedule here."

"Oh, come on," said Ivy. "Nothing can be that important. Have another drink, and then we can all go to the casino together."

"Tell you what," said Frank as he signaled for our check. "We'll see how the evening goes—and maybe we can meet up at the casino a little later."

****

Frank and I excused ourselves and left Ivy and Mark at the restaurant. Then, as soon as we were in his car, he returned to the subject I had been avoiding .

"So tell me," he said, "what did you decide—about Jillian's wedding?"

"Umm." I stalled while I searched for my seat belt.

"Tracy, I really need to let her know."

"Okay," I said, "I will go."

"Great. Thank you."

"But there is one condition."

He pulled away from the curb and headed toward the river. "What is your one condition?"

"Just this. Please don't try to include me in any of the photos. The whole thing will be awkward enough without that added stress."

"Sure, no problem," he said. "But I don't see it as being an issue. As an ex-husband, I doubt very much that even I will be drafted for any of the photos."

"Okay, good. But what are you going to wear?"

"Probably a pair of dress pants and my sport coat—if I can fit into it."

"You men have it so easy."

"Yes, we do. So, how about you?"

"Not so easy. Jewell vetoed everything I own and says we have to go dress shopping—in Grand Rapids."

"Sorry to complicate your life. But, if Jewell says so, it must be true."

"And of course Brooke wants to go along."

"And I'm sure the three of you will make a good choice. Do you want to borrow my credit card?"

"Oh, I don't think so—but it is sweet of you to offer."

"I realize that you're doing this for me."

"And don't you forget it, Buster."

"I won't." He reached out and squeezed my hand as we approached the highway. "Where would you like to go now?"

"Anywhere but the casino."

"Agreed. Let's go south. We can grab a drink somewhere in Ludington."

So that's what we did. And for the rest of the evening I never gave another thought to Ivy or Mark. I did, however, think quite a bit about the upcoming wedding.

The next day I called Jewell. "Well, I did it," I said. "I promised Frank I'd go with him to Jillian's wedding."

"Good for you, Tracy. I know he didn't want to go without you."

"Right. So now I have to go ahead with that dress shopping trip."

"Lighten up. I'll drive if you like. But we need to do it this Saturday, because Paul and I have people coming to visit for two weekends after that."

"Isn't it great to live in a beach town?"

"Oh sure, nobody knows we exist until summer comes around. Then everybody loves us."

"I'll plan on Saturday. I doubt if Brooke can get off on such short notice, but I'll tell her about it."

"Did I hear my name mentioned?" Brooke strolled into the living room just as I hung up.

"Yes, you did, and next Saturday is the shopping trip to Grand Rapids."

"Shopping—for your dress?"

"Yep. Do you want to go with us?"

"Of course I want to."

"But can you get off work?"

"Oh sure, I'll trade with someone." She headed for the kitchen, then turned around and said, "I just remembered. I took a phone call for you Friday."

"Anyone I know?"

"Actually, it was somebody at the paper. The call was about a guy trying to reach you. I wrote it down somewhere."

This struck me as a little odd, but not completely. If an unknown person tried to call me at work, especially if the caller was male, the staff usually did not give out my phone number, but would take contact information and pass it on to me. Brooke located a crumpled envelope and handed it to me. It took me a few seconds to make out the scribbled message. It read: *Tracy, please contact George Antonelli at this number...*

George Antonelli? Why on earth was this man trying to contact me? The only time I had seen the guy was that night at the yacht club when he was with his son Mark. Thinking back, I remembered that he had insisted on buying me drinks—maybe I should have refused. But then Frank showed up, so it should have been crystal clear that I was in a relationship.

But of course George Antonelli had bought the drinks before Frank appeared. And later that evening, Frank had wondered if maybe the guy was coming on to me—and I had insisted that Frank was wrong. After all, the guy was old enough to be my father.

So why was he calling me now?

CHAPTER TWENTY-SIX

"Well, that was a royal waste of time, not to mention taxpayer dollars," said Benny Dupree as he eased the sheriff's cruiser onto US 31 and entered Cedar County.

"You mean you didn't learn anything new about making methamphetamine?" said Frank.

"Not a damn thing," said the sheriff. "We knew it was a problem before we even left town. Hearing a bunch of statistics isn't doing us any good. And as far as coordinating with the state police, I think we do pretty good with that."

"At least we were able to escape after lunch," said Frank. "Everybody thought we were going to one of the seminars."

"I just couldn't sit still any longer," said Benny. "So tell me, any developments on our dead swimmer? You were going to track down the sister—what was her name?"

"The sister's name is Zoe. Her mother said she's got a summer job in Lansing and she's living there with some roommates. The mom gave me a phone number, but it's a landline, and every time I call, I seem to reach a different person who tells me that Zoe's not at home and they don't know when she will be."

"Think she's avoiding you?"

"I got the feeling that she really cared about her brother, so it seems like she would want to help."

"Goddammitall," Benny said as he slammed on his brakes. "Look at that."

As Benny slowed the cruiser, they joined a line of vehicles forming behind a trailer loaded with a super-wide structure that took up a lane and a half.

Traffic continued to crawl, and Benny continued to curse.

After about ten minutes, Frank said, "I think I figured out what's causing the slowdown. If I'm right, they'll be off the highway soon."

"So what the hell is it?"

"I got a glimpse of a sign that said Excelsior Entertainment, so I'd say they're heading for the Roxberry turnoff and it's for that music festival."

"Oh shit. Weeks off, and that thing is already causing problems."

"True—but the township gave them the permit, and I think you signed off on it."

"Guess I did. Every gas station in the county loves that week, so I didn't want to make them mad. But the damn thing seems to get bigger every year." Frank was proved right when the behemoth in front of them pulled off the main road and headed for the Rocking R Resort.

"Thank god," said Benny as he resumed speed. "Hey, what time is it anyway?"

"Little after three."

"Got anything going back in town?"

"Just paperwork. Try some phone calls."

"Then I'm gonna stop at the hospital and see if I can find Dr. Nancy."

"You and Nancy got a thing going?"

"Hah—very funny. Fact is, she called me. Said she needed to talk and she wanted to do it in person."

"Like I said—"

"No comment."

When they reached the hospital, Benny parked in the doctors' parking lot and the two men walked into the emergency room. The room was empty except for a tall guy in scrubs behind the desk. It was the ER supervisor, Don Fairchild.

"Hey," said Don when he saw them. "It's the long arm of the law. What can we do for you?"

"Looking for Dr. Nancy," said Benny. "Is she around?"

"She's on today," said Don, "and she shouldn't be hard to find. Just walked over to X-ray."

Seconds later, Dr. Nancy Peterman appeared. Her hair was raspberry red and sported a new style, short on the sides and spiked on top. "Well, hello, you two," she said when she saw Benny and Frank. "Don't tell me you guys caught a dose of that clap that's goin' around. I told you to be careful."

"If we did, Nancy, we'd be sure to bring it to you," said Frank.

"In this case, I believe you called me," said Benny.

"So I did," she replied. "Tell you what. I'm due for a coffee break. How about you guys join me?"

"Lead on," said Frank. He and Benny followed Dr. Nancy through a series of hallways to the cafeteria. Once inside, they each filled a cup from the coffee urn, the doctor got a slice of lemon pie and they sat at a table in the otherwise empty room. She dug into the pie and then got straight to the point.

"As you know," she said, "I am the medical examiner for Cedar County."

"Yep," said Benny. "Doc Mulligan was quite happy when you came along and took the job off his hands."

"Which was about a year ago."

"Guess you've had a fairly quiet year," said Benny, "except for a few drug overdoses."

"Right," she said, "but now I've come across something that's not in the manual, so I decided to run it by you. I had a visit from Jerry Whitmore. You know who that is?"

"We know Jerry," said Frank. "He's a detective with the state police."

"Right. Jerry was here, and he talked to me about signing off on a death certificate. It concerns a woman from Westerville who went missing nearly eight years ago."

"The timing makes sense," said Frank. "If a person goes missing but there is no body, they can't be declared dead until seven years later."

"I understand that," said Dr. Nancy. "But I'm new to this area, so I don't know anything about this case. Were either of you around seven years ago?"

"I was," said Benny. "I was a deputy back then."

"Ever hear of Hazel Everham?"

"Sure," said Benny. "She and her husband Everett ran an operation out there called the Everham Pork Farm."

"I looked that up," said Dr. Nancy. "They ran the business for fifteen years and then she went missing. About a year later, the whole thing closed down. I understand the place is empty."

"It is," said Benny. "I heard that he moved out west somewhere. And now somebody wants a death certificate?"

"Right. Somebody out in Oregon."

"Is it her husband," said Frank, "trying to collect life insurance?"

"It's not about insurance," she said. "It's about her death. Jerry said he got a tip from a county sheriff out in Oregon about Everett Everham. Word is that he tends to drink a lot."

"That's no surprise," said Benny.

"And here's what got their attention," said the doctor. "Sometimes when he's drunk, Everett brags about how he killed his wife back in Michigan. And got away with it."

CHAPTER TWENTY-SEVEN

"I kind of liked that last dress I tried on," I said.

"No way," said Brooke. "That thing made you look like a walrus."

Jewell was a little more tactful. "I just don't think black is a good color for a wedding."

"It wasn't all black," I said. "It had those flowers across the top."

The great shopping trip was under way. The purpose, of course, was to dress me in a manner befitting attendance at the wedding of Frank's ex-wife. It was almost noon when we arrived at the mall, so we had visited only one store before taking a break for lunch.

The dress discussion went on hiatus while the waitress delivered a grilled cheese sandwich for Brooke and tuna salads for Jewell and me. Brooke struggled to stifle a yawn as she pointed to her coffee cup and requested a refill.

"Guess you got home a bit late last night," I said.

"Yes, it was late," she said with another yawn, this one unstifled. "I told Scott I wanted an early night, but he insisted on going to the casino. Then, when we got home, he wanted to stay over—and I had already told him that wasn't going to happen because I had this shopping trip coming up."

"So that's what I heard last night."

"Yes, it was us arguing, and I'm sorry. I didn't mean to wake you up."

"No problem. I pretty much went right back to sleep."

"Good. And I'm glad to be here. I wasn't going to let anything make me miss this shopping trip."

"It is definitely a rare occasion," said Jewell, "taking Tracy dress shopping."

"Pretty much once in a lifetime," said Brooke.

"Point taken," I said. "I don't like shopping, so I don't do it much. But shopping with you two makes it almost enjoyable. I'm just sorry that Sara couldn't bring the grandbaby for lunch."

"Me too," said Jewell, "but the only thing more disruptive that a toddler at lunch is a toddler with a messy head cold." She put down her fork. "Now, back to Tracy's dress. I spotted three more shops right here in the mall, and they all look promising."

"You know," I said, "my trouble with dresses is that I'm tall. So the waistline always shows up in the wrong place."

"And that's why you want to wear a tent?" said Brooke. "You don't need to do that."

"There are other solutions," said Jewell. "A lot of shirring around the waist. Or a dress made in two pieces."

"Or that other thing," said Brooke, "the empire waist."

"Veto that," I said. "Those only look good on women who are five feet tall."

"We'll just keep looking," said Jewell. "And I spotted a couple of shoe stores too."

After lunch, we visited all of the stores that Jewell had spotted, where I tried on more dresses than I can recall. The three-way mirror was a bit scary, and the whole process exhausting but, after a while, I was able to relax and let my friends wait on me.

Finally, we found a store that seemed to cater to grown women, and it was there that we narrowed the field to three candidates. One was yellow with something called a peplum.

"No dice," I said, once I had it on. "This reminds me of Marge."

The next one was green with a mermaid-style skirt. I vetoed the color. "This makes me look jaundiced." The final candidate featured a gauzy material in aquamarine. It had a light blue ruffle across the bust—plus, it fit nicely across my middle and the skirt covered my knees.

"This looks good," I said. "But I need to see what happens when I sit down." So I sat. This caused the skirt to ride up. "Am I showing too much thigh?"

"Hardly any," said Jewell.

"I think this is it," I said.

Jewell made me stand and turn around a few times before she agreed.

"Hurray," said Brooke. "Now we can look for shoes."

"Do we have to?" I said.

"Oh, come on," said Jewell. "You can't go to the wedding in sneakers."

"Or your Birkenstocks," said Brooke.

"But I'm exhausted. Shopping is hard work."

"I know what you need," said Jewell. "Let's take a break and have some coffee."

"And chocolate cake," said Brooke.

So that's what we did. And then we went shoe shopping.

****

It was after seven when the three of us got back to town, and I was the proud owner of a new blue dress and a pair of something called espadrilles with two-inch wedge heels.

I invited Jewell to come in and have something to eat, but she declined. So Brooke and I told her goodnight, went inside and headed for the kitchen to see what we could find for supper.

"I see we have messages," Brooke said as she passed by the answering machine. "Shall I play them?"

"Sure, go ahead. Might be Frank." Brooke pushed the play button. The first message was from Scott: "Hey, Brooke, thought I'd see if you wanted to do something tonight."

"Ignore that," she said.

The second message was from a man, but it was not Frank. "This is George Antonelli calling for Tracy Quinn—please give me a call at—"

"We'll ignore that one too," I said.

CHAPTER TWENTY-EIGHT

Frank was in his office Monday morning when he had a call from Zoe Braxton, the sister of their drowning victim. "I'm working at The Holiday House," she said. "It's a restaurant in East Lansing. If you meet me there on my lunch hour, we can talk."

"Sounds good," said Frank. "Can we do it tomorrow?"

"That would be okay." Zoe gave him directions. "My break is at twelve thirty."

"Where should I look for you?"

"We have tables outside. I'll be there, on the south side."

"Right. Do you still have blue hair?"

"Yes. And you're the guy I met at my parents' house?"

"That's me—six two and overweight."

She laughed. "Okay then, see you tomorrow."

Frank ended the call just as the sheriff came through the door. "Congratulate me," said Frank. "I just managed to track down the sister."

"What sister?"

"Zoe Braxton—her brother was our body on the beach."

"I hope you make some progress," said Benny. "It's getting so I can't walk the street without someone wantin' to know exactly what happened to that boy. Lucy Perkins cornered me yesterday and said the chamber of commerce is worried that an unsolved murder is going to frighten away summer visitors."

"I'll do my best. Want to come with me tomorrow?"

"No, I'm gonna make a trip out to Hesperia—something about an illegal dog kennel."

The next day Frank drove to East Lansing and it was not yet noon when he located the Holiday House, ouse a sprawling one-story building with an equally sprawling parking lot. He swung by a fast-food place and got a coffee to go, then returned to the restaurant and parked where he could keep an eye on the south exit.

Before long, he saw a tall girl wearing black shorts and a white shirt emerge; her hair was unmistakably blue. He got out of his car and waited. She looked around and waved when she saw him. He walked over and they shook hands. Zoe led Frank to a table under an umbrella. "I need the shade today," she explained. "I spent yesterday at the beach, and I think I overdid it a little."

Zoe was holding a tumbler of ice water and Frank still had his coffee. They sat at the table. "First of all," he said, "tell me about your family. Are there any other siblings?"

"No, there were just the two of us. Tony is—Tony was— four years older than me."

"So you and Tony grew up together?"

"Yep, I was the baby sister, and I really looked up to him. Tony was pretty good to me, at least most of the time." She took out a tissue and blew her nose. "I'm sorry."

"No problem," he said. "Take your time. How are your parents coping?"

"Not well. I think my dad's drinking again."

"That's too bad. But tell me—when was the last time you saw your brother?"

"I've been thinking about that. Maybe a month before he died. I didn't see him a lot because he spent so much time with Brandi—you know how it is, when two people are infatuated, they don't really need anyone else. You knew about Brandi, didn't you?"

"Yes, I did. In fact I met her because she came to the morgue to identify him."

"So he didn't have his license or wallet or anything?"

"No. We did find his clothes a few days later, but there was no wallet or any other ID."

"So somebody must have his stuff."

"Looks that way. Either that or it somehow got lost in the sand. We had a big storm about a week later. How long had Brandi and your brother been together?"

"Not all that long. Maybe six months."

"Did he have another girlfriend before Brandi?"

"He dated a little, but I don't remember that he was ever serious about anyone."

"She told us they were planning to get married," said Frank, "so that would mean their relationship, ah, developed pretty fast."

"It did. For both of them—but especially for Brandi, I think. Her love life, I believe, was a little more complicated."

"How so?"

"Someone told me that Brandi had been pretty steady with another guy—until she met Tony. But after that, well, she changed gears pretty fast. Nothing against Brandi. I guess she met my brother, fell hard, and decided that he was the one."

Frank scribbled a few notes but mostly listened. He remembered one of the many theories about this death had included a love triangle.

"Do you know who this other guy was?"

"I don't think I ever heard a name."

"Do you think you could find out who it was?"

"I can certainly ask around."

"If you find out, would you let me know?" He handed her his business card.

"Sure, I'm glad to help," she said. "The funeral is coming up Saturday, and Brandi will be there. Along with a lot of her friends."

CHAPTER TWENTY-NINE

Tracy, theirs a guy out front waiting to see you.

I found the note taped to my computer when I arrived at the office Monday after a road commission meeting. I could tell that the note was written by Tiffany, our newest hire in the front office. We all knew that spelling was not her strong suit.

I wondered who the guy might be while I turned on the computer and reviewed my notes. I was hoping to get the piece finished before I broke for lunch. But my plans were interrupted by a visit from Tiffany herself.

"Tracy," she said, "the guy is out here waiting. And Sylvia told him you would be coming in before noon."

"Isn't there anyone else who can handle this?"

"Nope. He said he had to talk to you."

"Do you know who it is?"

"Don't know him. Grey hair but kind of nice looking—for an old guy."

"Okay," I said. "Tell him I'll be out in a minute." I grumbled and stalled but finally waltzed out to the front office where I spotted a man on the far side of the room, viewing the historic photos on the wall. Then he turned around. Perhaps I shouldn't have been surprised to see that it was George Antonelli.

"Ms. Quinn," he said. "I've been trying to reach you."

"Oh yes, I've been—well, I've been really busy."

"I only need a few minutes of your time," he said. "But I need to talk in private."

I looked across the street, at the Village Grounds Coffee Shop. "Let's go over there," I said. "I could use an iced coffee."

"Great," he replied. "And thank you."

I told Tiffany I'd be back in a few minutes and accompanied George Antonelli across the street. Minutes later we were inside, seated at a corner table with our drinks. "I'm sorry I've been reduced to stalking you," he said, "but the fact is, I need to tell you something— about my son."

"Your son, Mark?"

"Yes, the one who's been seeing your friend Ivy."

"Okay, sure. What about him?"

"She needs to know that Mark is—well, he's married."

"Hmm. I guess she hasn't mentioned that."

"Probably because she doesn't know. And that's because he tends to not divulge his marital status. The truth is that he's not separated, he's not divorcing, and they don't have an open marriage. He has a wife and family in Chicago, and he's just plain cheating."

"You think I should tell her?"

"I'm asking you to tell her. It's important."

"Why?"

George Antonelli took a moment with his drink. "I'll try to make a long story short," he said. "This is Mark's second marriage, and he's always been unfaithful. I don't know where he learned it from; it's not my style." I nodded, suppressing my urge to take notes. It's a reporter thing.

"Over the years I've tried to ignore the whole issue. To act like it was none of my business—but then he became involved with a girl named Sarah. Sarah was young, she was in love, and she believed all his lies. It went on for two years, and when she finally found out..." He stopped, and covered his face with his hands. Then he looked up and said, "When Sarah found out, she committed suicide."

I don't know what I had expected, but it wasn't this. "Ooh," was all I could say. "How sad—"

"It was terrible. Not everybody knew the whole story, but I eventually pieced it all together. And that was the one time I talked to him about — his selfishness—his disregard for the consequences of his actions. But I might as well have been talking to a wall. He said that Sarah was unstable and pretended that her death had nothing to do with him."

"Sounds pretty cold."

"Cold is right. But still I was hoping that maybe the tragedy would cause him to change his ways. And I thought maybe he had, until I saw him with your friend Ivy. Now I know he hasn't changed a bit; he's at it again."

"So—you want me to tell Ivy what, exactly?"

"Tell her that Mark is married with two little kids. And when he's not chasing around Michigan, he lives with his family in Chicago."

I told George Mark's father I would do what he asked. But I was already dreading the conversation with Ivy.

CHAPTER THIRTY

"Wasn't it you who said our body on the beach might have something to do with a love triangle?"

"Not me," said Benny. "Hey, this is pretty good."

Frank and Benny were in the sheriff's office having their morning coffee break. Benny was sampling a strawberry Danish and Frank had a chocolate donut, all compliments of the new bakery in town. They were also comparing notes on their solo investigations.

Frank persisted. "I'm pretty sure the triangle theory came from you, Benny. You said you heard it from a girl reporter, in this case, Ivy Martin."

"Then I guess it was me. So what?"

"I had a talk with the victim's sister."

"That was your trip to Lansing. Did you find out anything?"

"Maybe. First of all, remember Brandi, the girlfriend of the dead guy? The one who came to the morgue."

"I remember. Kind of short with curly hair."

"That's the one." Frank wiped chocolate from his fingers. "Well, Zoe, that's the sister, told me something. Zoe said that before Brandi and Scott got together—before Brandi met Scott—she had another boyfriend."

"Hmm. So let me see if I track this. You're saying that if there was another guy in the picture—that would create a triangle?"

"Looks that way to me."

"Okay, could be. So who was this other guy?"

"We don't know yet," said Frank. "But Zoe said she would find out for me. At the funeral."

"Okay, good," said the sheriff. "But now we've got this request from Dr. Nancy."

"Someone wants her to sign a death certificate," said Frank. "And that seems a little unusual, coming from Oregon. What will you do?"

"I told Dr. Nancy to go ahead and sign the certificate and I would check our file on the missing woman." Benny moved his coffee and made room on his desk for a manila folder. The label said *Hazel Everham*.

"Looks pretty sparse," said Frank as he opened the folder.

"Neighbors reported her missing," said Benny. "And the husband said his wife went to Texas to visit her sister .. but never came back. The last entry was about three years after she went missing."

Frank perused the file. "According to this, the sister, whose name is Jennie, said Hazel never came to Texas. In fact, Jennie never saw Hazel again and never even got a Christmas card from her. Have you tried to call this sister?"

"I tried yesterday," said Benny. "But the number isn't in service."

"Dead end there. Did the couple have any children?"

"There was one son," said Benny. "I remember how he died. When he finished high school, the parents bought him a car and he celebrated by getting drunk and wrapping it around a tree."

"Sad story. So there's no one else we can ask about her?"

"Yes and no. There certainly would be neighbors."

"Maybe we should take a ride out to Westerville," said Frank.

"Let's do it," said Benny.

Twenty minutes later they were in Benny's cruiser headed east and Frank was paging through a tattered plat book. "You know how to use that?" said Benny.

"Sure I do. But isn't this thing pretty old?"

"It is. But remember, we're looking for the farm that Everham owned eight years ago."

"Oh sure, that makes sense. So turn left at the next crossroad."

With a little cursing and a lot of squinting at the book's fine print, the men located what appeared to be the old pig farm. The two-story house was flaking green paint and had several broken windows. In the yard a For Sale sign swung crookedly on one chain.

"Looks like no one will mind if we snoop around a little." Benny turned onto the property. They followed a driveway that was well on its way to being overgrown. It led behind the house to a large wooden barn that had long ago lost any trace of paint. The barn was flanked by half a dozen smaller buildings, and Benny pointed out their distinctive hexagonal shape. "You can tell this was a pig farm," he said.

"How's that?"

"Those buildings with six sides," he said. "They're farrowing pens for the sows—the mother pigs, that is."

"Okay, I know what a sow is."

"Early spring, when it's still cold at night, the farmer puts his pregnant mamas in there with some kind of heat at the center, and that shape allows the heat to circulate. So more of the piggies survive."

"Well, now," said Frank, "that's something I didn't know."

"And did you know that a sow will eat a dead piglet?"

"Didn't know that."

"In fact pigs will eat just about anything."

"I'm getting a real education here."

"And probably it's all useless." Benny said as he headed back to the road. "Let's go into town and see if we can find anybody to talk to us." Entering the town of Westerville, they passed a sign proclaiming that the town had a population of five hundred, but they found no one at the village hall, the fire station, or even the library. The only grocery store had closed down.

"Got any ideas?" said Frank.

"Maybe," said Benny. "There's a tavern just north of town, and I seem to recall they have pretty good hamburgers."

"Let's hope they haven't closed down."

"I'm pretty sure the place is open," said Benny. "Only last month we sent a couple of deputies out there to handle a brawl." Benny was right. The Crystal Creek Tavern was open and having its noon rush, which meant there were four customers in the place, with Frank and Benny bringing that number up to six.

Once inside, Benny introduced Frank to the owner, Milt Granger, who was tending bar and waiting tables. Milt was short and obese, dressed in striped overalls and a grimy looking baseball cap.

"Hey, Milt, is your wife in the kitchen?" said Benny.

"Yep, Edna is doing the honors."

"In that case, we'll have a couple of burgers. I don't trust anyone except Edna. And afterward, we'd like to pick your brain a little."

Milt yelled the order into the kitchen while the two men seated themselves. "Not sure how much I can help," he said as he brought them coffee.

"Guess you've had this place a long time," said Benny.

"Over twenty years."

"We wanted ask about the couple that had that pig farm south of town."

"Sounds like you're talking about Everett and Hazel Everham."

"Yep, remember them?"

"Sure do," said Milt. "Can't say I was sorry to see them go."

"Why was that?"

"They came in here a lot—and generally behaved okay during the week. But then, every Saturday night like clockwork, the two of them would show up and he'd start drinking shots. Pretty soon he'd be plastered—I mean, real belligerent—then they'd argue and he'd start to rough her up until someone stopped him."

"Burgers ready," came a voice from the kitchen.

"Coming!" he yelled back. To the men he said, "Edna always said that if Hazel walked out on that guy, she had good reason."

"Do you think that's what happened?" said Benny.

Milt paused, rubbed his whiskered chin. "No, I don't think so," he said. "And neither does Edna. Fact is, we always felt like somebody ought to take a closer look at that whole mess."

CHAPTER THIRTY-ONE

"Why, that detestable, lying snake," said Ivy. "Just wait till I get my hands on him."

As anticipated, Ivy Martin was not reacting well to the news about her current love interest, Mark Antonelli.

It had been almost a week since George Antonelli tracked me down to inform me that his son was married—married and fooling around, making Ivy the other woman. One might say I had been putting off the encounter, or one might say that I simply hadn't had the opportunity for a private chat. But now, here we were, at the chamber of commerce event called "After Hours Meet and Greet" which was taking place at the Seagull Bar and Grill.

The turnout was good, and we were part of the overflow that had moved outside onto the patio. The patio had its own bar and Ivy and I were seated at the far end, with no one paying us much attention, not even the barkeep. That's when I went ahead and gave her the bad news about Mark.

"But Tracy, are you absolutely sure about this?"

"Ivy, I'm not a hundred percent sure of anything. I only know what Mark's father told me. That said, I don't see any reason for him to lie."

"But Mark was talking, honest to gosh, he talked about moving to Michigan so we could see more of each other. Maybe even live together."

"News flash, Ivy. People lie. All the time."

"I guess it's possible, but, I mean, what a blow. And coming from you, Tracy, of all people. I thought you were my friend."

"Come on, Ivy, don't shoot the messenger."

She took a sip of her tequila sunset and looked thoughtful. "Now that Mark is back in Chicago, he calls me almost every day. I'd like to find out for sure."

"What about phone calls? That business card he gave us? Doesn't it have more than one phone number?"

Ivy was quiet for a moment. "You know, I think he has two cell phones. I found a second one in his coat pocket and asked him about it...he said not to mess with it, it was strictly for business calls."

"So one for business," I said, "and one for monkey business."

"Or one for me and one for the wife."

"Guess that could be the case."

"Come to think of it," she said, "I have heard Mark mention his kids—but I was sure he said the mother was his ex-wife."

"And that could be from his first marriage. George said he's on his second, or maybe third."

"Well, crap." Ivy took a swallow of her drink. "But maybe—maybe they have an open marriage."

"George said that's one of the stories he likes to use."

"But Mark seems like such—such a sincere, honest person."

That's when I, reluctantly, decided to go ahead and tell Ivy about Mark's affair with the girl named Sarah. Ivy was quiet while she emptied her drink and signaled for another. I finished up the sad tale. "When Sarah found out he was married and had no plans to divorce, she, well, she committed suicide."

"Oh, that is sad." Ivy accepted her drink from the bartender and flashed him a smile. "Then I guess he really is a snake."

"It sure looks that way."

"What do you think I should do?"

This was a first. Ivy had never before asked me for advice on her love life. "I can't tell you what to do," I said. "That's your decision—but George was adamant that you needed to know."

Ivy scrunched up her face as she removed the umbrella from her drink. She twirled the little parasol a few times before she tossed it aside. Then she then picked up the glass and drank it all down. When she was finished, a look of satisfaction spread over her face. "Tell you what I'm gonna do," she said. "I'm gonna get even with that lying creep."

"I'm sure you will, Ivy. I have complete faith in you."

"Want to hear my plan?"

"Sure. I mean, I guess so." *But did I really want to know?* If Ivy's plan included murder, I figured I should make an effort to change her mind. Would I be some kind of accessory if I didn't? But I needn't have worried. When she told me her scheme, I was relieved to learn that it wasn't anything illegal or even violent. Her revenge plot included neither of these elements—but it was typical Ivy.

In a familiar gesture, she pushed that long hair back from her forehead and said, "I wonder how Mark would like it if I seduced his father."

CHAPTER THIRTY-TWO

The weather was warm with a slight breeze, making a perfect day for an outdoor wedding. The bride wore an ivory satin dress with lace at the neckline and carried a bouquet of tiger lilies. She was escorted down the aisle by her two grandsons...who wore matching tuxedoes with yellow bow ties.

I was writing up the event in my head, which was the best way I could think of to cope with being Frank's date at the wedding of his ex-wife Jillian. I had insisted that we sit in the back and that worked out fine, since those were the only seats left when we made our slightly tardy entrance.

When the brief ceremony was over, the newlywed couple headed down the aisle and I got a look at the groom. Not too bad. In size, a lot like Frank—so Jillian had a type, maybe. But where Frank was dark-haired, this guy was blonde going gray.

I had told Frank I definitely would not stay for the reception—in fact, that had been one of my conditions. But now there was the unmistakable sound of corks popping as guests left their seats and reassembled in a tent directly behind us. Frank squeezed my hand. "Want to have some champagne before we go?"

"Okay, I guess."

"After all, we drove a long way."

"Yes, we did." So we got in line for champagne, and the couple in front of us greeted Frank. He introduced them, and I learned that the couple was Tom and Amy.

"And this is my lady friend, Tracy Quinn," Frank said. "I keep asking her to marry me, but so far, no luck."

His declaration was not exactly true, but it was definitely flattering. We all laughed, and I was still shaking hands with Amy when I heard excited cries of, "Grampa, Grampa!"

Of course I knew that Frank had a daughter who had two children—I knew he was a grandfather. But it still struck me as strange to hear him addressed as such by this boisterous pair. They came running toward us, cummerbunds twisted and bowties askew. Frank greeted them with hugs and managed to pick up the smaller one.

"Tracy," he said, "these two hoodlums are Pete and Lucas. And boys, this is—"

"You have to sit with us," cried the bigger one. "We have a special table."

"With our names on it—and your names too."

Frank looked at me over Pete's head with a helpless expression. And that's when I knew we would not be leaving this event any time soon. So I put on my best face and smiled as I was introduced to people whose names I promptly forgot. I met Frank's son and remembered that his name was Lincoln. I was on my second glass of champagne when the boys led us to a round table set for six in the reception tent.

"We're gonna have shrimp cocktail," said Lucas.

"And raspberry chocolate cake," said Pete.

The boys pointed out name cards at the table for Frank and me, and for themselves. All this time Pete and Lucas stayed pretty close to Frank, sometimes hanging on to his hands. When the emcee asked us all to take seats, our table was completed by Frank's daughter Sandra and a man who was either her husband or her boyfriend...but anyway, his name was Cade. There was a large bottle of zinfandel on the table, and Cade won my approval when he opened it and began to pour.

The shrimp cocktail arrived as promised. Luke looked a bit disappointed, as though he might have expected it to be a drink. We had tropical fruit salad followed by curried okra and then a seafood combo over rice. "It's called jambalaya," Sandra said by way of explaining the menu. "The groom was raised in Louisiana."

"The food is all great," I said, and I meant it.

"And there will be no speeches," said Sandra.

"Thanks goodness for that," Frank whispered to me.

There was, however, a band. Several musicians arrived and proceeded to set up their equipment on the plywood stage. When the band was ready, the couple was called out for their first dance, and I had to admit they did look nice together. That's when Frank's daughter Sandra made an announcement, but only to our table.

"When I was in junior high, we had a father-daughter dance, but Dad couldn't make it. So now"—she reached out and grabbed him by his necktie—"now he's going to make it up to me."

And just like that, Frank was out on the dance floor. Somebody asked Cade to come and help with an electrical problem, and that left me with Frank's two grandsons. I'll give the boys credit. They did their best to engage me in conversation.

"Do you like being a reporter?"

"Yes, I do, it's—"

"Are you ever on television?"

"Well, no, but—"

"Are you and Grampa gonna get married?"

The table went silent with four eyes fastened on me and four freshly scrubbed ears waiting for an answer. I decided to punt. "I keep asking him," I said solemnly. "But so far, well, he just can't make up his mind."

I was rescued from that subject by a rather elegant woman with silver hair who told the boys they were supposed to help her with a project. "And remember," she said, "it's a secret."

The boys both disappeared with her.

Which left me in the position I had dreaded all along—sitting alone at the table. I had a limited view of the dance floor and noticed that when Frank and his daughter finished their dance, he headed back to our table. But he never made it because he was waylaid by a blonde in a clingy red dress. And it wasn't just the dress that was clingy. She soon had Frank in a lock, with her arms around his neck as she favored him with a frozen smile, the kind that comes after cosmetic surgery. I couldn't tell if he was enjoying the attention or not, but I decided not to add to the spectacle by staring at them.

Instead I contemplated my empty wine glass and was considering another piece of cake when I heard a male voice saying, "Hey, mind if I sit down?"

I looked up and discovered a man who looked to be about my age, sporting a yellow shirt and a flowered necktie. He also looked the tiniest bit familiar. "Sure," I said, "glad to have company." And I really was.

"Aren't you Tracy?" he said as he slid onto the chair next to mine.

"Guilty as charged." I took a closer look at my new friend. His hair was mostly gray, but the red moustache gave him away. "Well, darn it all, you must be...Sam."

"Yes, that's me."

I had known Sam Larston while we were both in college, but I hadn't seen him since we graduated, some twenty plus years ago. "Tracy, you're looking great. You haven't changed a bit."

"Thanks for the lie, Sam. You're looking pretty good yourself."

"So, what are you doing here?"

"Long story short," I said, "I'm here with my boyfriend. He is, well, he's part of this family, and he seems to be ignoring me."

"Interesting. I have sort of the same situation."

"Girlfriend ignoring you?"

"Not quite—"

"Aha, boyfriend ignoring you?"

"You got it."

"You know, Sam, you were always so easy to be around that sometimes I wondered a little."

"And I thought about coming out, but, well, it was twenty years ago, and things were different."

"Yes, and isn't it great that some things in this world have changed for the better?"

"Absolutely. Hey, would you like to dance?"

****

"So who was that guy you spent so much time with on the dance floor?" Frank lobbed the question at me as we were on our way home, after staying longer than intended at the wedding reception.

"Maybe I'll tell you about him," I said, "but only after you explain the blonde in the red dress who had such designs on you."

He laughed. "Okay, that was Lucinda. She was family."

"She wasn't acting like your sister."

"Sister-in-law. She was married to Jillian's brother. They divorced about the same time we did, so she figured the two of us were due for an affair."

"So did you?"

"No way." Frank emitted a sound best described as a snort.

"Why not?"

"Two reasons. First of all, I never liked her much. She loved to say nasty things about people...sometimes they were true and sometimes not. Never really mattered matter to her."

"And reason number two?"

"I didn't need any more drama with that family. That's one reason I got out of town as quick as I could."

"And moved to Cedar County?"

"That's right. And it's been a good move."

"Worked out well for me."

"So, now tell me about the guy you were dancing with."

"Oh sure. Well, that was Sam. We were in college together."

"Did you two date?"

"We were good friends." I thought about pretending that Sam and I had been a hot item but decided there was nothing to be gained by deception. "But Sam was—still is—gay."

"Oh. So much for my gaydar. Guess that means I don't need to be jealous."

"Not a bit."

"Anyway, thanks for hanging around. You look great in that dress and I'm sorry you got left alone at times."

"I managed. And by the way, you and the boys looked pretty good out there doing the hokey pokey."

"Thanks," he said. "And I'm glad you could tolerate those two, because I promised to bring them for an overnight at my place."

"Oh, that should be interesting."

"That's for sure. Especially since I promised it would be a campout. I said we would put up tents in the woods behind my cabin."

"City boys," I said with a laugh. "Just wait until they hear a hoot from that owl." After that we were didn't talk much and I was almost asleep when we arrived back in town. But Frank's next comment woke me up. .

"Take a look," he said. "There seems to be some excitement at your house."

******

Looking up, I saw two cars parked on the street in front of my house and one of them was a police car, complete with flashing blue-and-white lights. "Looks like you're right," I said.

"Can't be too serious," said Frank. "It's one of the village cops."

We both knew that the village had a chief of police but didn't maintain a full-time force, except in the summer, when the overflow of tourists created problems related to parking spaces.

"And I think the other car belongs to our friend Scott," I said. When we parked behind the cop car, I saw three figures standing on the street. One of them broke away and walked in our direction. It was Brooke.

"Hey, glad you guys are here," she said.

"What's going on?" said Frank.

"Oh, someone decided Scott needed to be harassed. You'd have thought we robbed a bank or something. But, as it turned out, it's all about a missing tail light."

"That's enough to get their attention," said Frank.

"So now it's, you know, we have to go through the whole business of, show me your license, the car insurance, and all the paperwork."

"That's the routine," said Frank.

"I guess Scott managed to show the police officer everything he wants to see."

"Then the guy will probably let him off with a warning to fix the light." At this point Frank stepped forward and made his presence known to the young policeman.

"I hope Frank just tells the guy to buzz off," said Brooke.

"Probably not," I said. "That's not his style."

I was right. Frank did not interfere as the process moved toward its conclusion. Brooke and I watched as Scott signed a paper and the young policeman gave him a copy. Then the cop wished us all a good evening, got in his car, and pulled away.

"Glad that's over," said Scott, as he folded the paper and stuck it in his rear pocket. I thought maybe his hand was shaking.

"Me too," said Brooke. "Do you want to come inside?"

"No way," he said. "I need to get going."

"Okay," said Brooke. She gave him a brief hug, then turned and headed for the house.

"See you guys later," Scott said to Frank and me, just before he jumped into his car and cranked it up.

"Seemed in a bit of a hurry," said Frank.

"Yes, he did," I said. "Usually he likes to hang around here as long as possible."

Frank and I went inside, where we found Brooke in the kitchen, munching on a chicken leg. "Other than the ending which we just witnessed," I said, "how was your evening?"

Brooke waved the cold drumstick at us. "The whole thing was a disaster. When he picked me up from work I told him I was tired and hungry. He said we'd just go to Ludington and have a burger, and I said fine."

"So did you?"

"No. Once I was in the car, he said there was a concert at the beach and we should go to that. I reminded him I was hungry, and he said no problem, there would be food for sale."

"And was there?"

"Oh, hell no. First of all, there was no place to park, so we had to walk at least a mile, and I was getting hungrier all the time. I ended up eating two popsicles for supper because that's all they had."

"So, not a great evening."

"Not a great evening. And then you saw how it ended. But hey, look at you in your gorgeous dress. How was the wedding?"

"The wedding was not too bad, actually."

"And that color looks great on you."

"Thanks, Brooke. And thanks for forcing me to go dress shopping. But what about Scott? Are you going to see him again?"

"I'd really like to wind things down. But now he's talking about tickets for that music festival."

"The thing looks to be really big," said Frank. "They're paying a lot of local law enforcement to be on hand. Plus, I heard that tickets are hard to find, and the ones available are getting expensive."

"Probably scalper rates," said Brooke. "But Scott said not to worry. He'd take care of everything."

"That's generous of him," said Frank.

"Yes and no," she replied. "Sometimes I don't like it when he insists on paying for everything. It makes me feel a little bit...I dunno..."

"Like a kept woman?" I suggested.

"Just not very independent." Brooke opened the refrigerator and found a slice of pizza. She popped the slice into the microwave, and while it was warming, her expression turned thoughtful. "You know what?" she said. "I just thought of something that happened tonight that seemed—kind of strange."

"What was that?"

"When the cop asked Scott for his driver's license, he started to hand it over and then said, 'oops, wrong one.' Scott took it back and actually gave him another one."

"Now, that does seem strange."

"Maybe he was carrying an expired license," I said.

"Maybe. But why would anybody carry around an old drivers license?"

CHAPTER THIRTY-THREE

"Some girl has been trying to call you," Sheriff Benny said to Frank when he arrived at the office Monday morning.

"Did she sound like she had blue hair?" said Frank.

"Possibly blue hair. But definitely young."

"Did she leave a number?"

"Yep, and here it is." Benny handed Frank a yellow sticky note.

"Thanks," Frank said as he took the paper and proceeded to punch in the number. "I'm hoping this will be Zoe, the sister of our drowning victim. She said the funeral would be Saturday and she was going to see what she could find out."

"What are you hoping to learn?"

"Anything I can," said Frank, "but specifically, she was going to find out who Brandi was dating before she got involved with our victim Tony."

"Who's Brandi?"

"Brandi is the girl Tony was planning to marry. Zoe told me that Brandi had been seeing another guy before she met Tony."

"So this guy would be—what?"

"The jilted lover," said Frank. "The jealous ex."

"Okay, it's possible. And, like you said, we don't really have any other good theories."

"And here's another thing," said Frank. "Now that I think about it— "

"What's that?"

"When Zoe was talking to her parents, they said things like, Tony couldn't possibly get married because he didn't have a job or a place to live."

"Or a pot to piss in," said Benny. "But kids are so dumb nowadays, that's how they do things."

"Okay. And that's when Zoe explained to her parents that if Tony and Brandi got married, her dad was going to provide Tony with a job, an apartment, maybe even a car. So she was sort of a package deal."

"So maybe this guy," said Benny, "whoever he was. Maybe he figured if Tony was out of the way—he might get the girl back, along with all the benefits."

"We don't seem to have any other leads," said Frank. "And didn't this idea come from you in the first place?"

"From me?"

"Yes, you. I believe you used the term *love triangle.*" The telephone rang and Frank picked up. "Cedar County Sheriff's office."

"Hi, I'm looking for Frank Kolowsky."

"You got him," said Frank. "Is this Zoe Braxton?"

"That's me," she said.

"So, I guess you were at your brother's funeral."

"Yep. That whole circus took place on Saturday."

"Can you tell me about it?"

"I can, but I'd rather not do it on the phone."

"Okay, do you want to meet up?"

"Sure. I'll be in Muskegon tomorrow. How about the McDonald's on Fortieth Street?"

"I can do that. What time?"

"Let's make it noon," she said.

"Great. I'll be there."

****

Zoe Braxton arrived early for their meeting. Frank found her waiting when he arrived, sitting at a table outside the restaurant. "Been waiting long?" he said as he approached.

"Just a few minutes," she said. "No problem."

Frank sat down across from her and saw that her eyes were red and swollen. Zoe sniffled and blew her nose. "Sorry," she said as she fumbled for a tissue.

"Take your time," he said. "Want some coffee?"

"No. I mean, yes—coffee might be good."

Frank went inside, got two coffees and sugar packets. When he returned to their table, Zoe thanked him and gave him a weak smile. "Their coffee tends to be scalding," he said as he handed her one of the cups. "So I slipped in an ice cube."

"And thank you for that." Zoe stirred in the sugar and took a sip. "Guess I'm ready now."

"Okay. Just start by telling me about the funeral."

"It was huge. Too big for the church or even the funeral home. They ended up using the high school gym."

"So it looks as though your brother was well liked."

"Sure, that was part of it. Tony did have a lot of friends. And so does Brandi. I think some of the people there didn't even know Tony, but they came to support Brandi. And that was okay—I'm sure she needed it. There were others I suspect just came for the drama. But maybe I'm being too hard on them." She stopped, took a deep breath and swallowed some coffee before she continued.

"Anyway, there was our family: grandparents and aunts, uncles and cousins—and then this mob of friends and just random people. Before the service started, a lot of them were congregated around Brandi, who was sobbing and moaning. It seemed like she enjoyed being the center of attention—but I shouldn't be too critical. She did love Tony."

"And did you talk to anyone who knew about—well, about Brandi's past, so to speak?"

"I did, as soon as I could slip away from my family. I think maybe I coped with my feelings by getting into spy mode. So I mingled with the young crowd and talked to a lot of people, mostly girls, until I found a couple of them who were eager to dish about Brandi's previous relationships."

"Good for you."

"I didn't trust my memory so, as soon as got away, I went ahead and wrote things down." Zoe reached into a pocket and pulled out a crumpled piece of paper. "So here you are, detective. I've got two names for you."

"Two names?"

"Yes, two. Actually, there were more than two, but these were the most recent. You see, Brandi, my almost-sister-in-law—it seems she had a rather complicated love life."

Frank took the paper, looked it over and slipped it into his little spiral notebook. "You've been a big help," he said. "Can I get you something to eat?"

CHAPTER THIRTY-FOUR

"Hey, this is a winner," I said to Brooke. "I don't think I've ever had white chili before."

"I haven't either," she said, "but I was looking through your grandma's cookbook and there it was, so I decided to give it a try."

"Well, it's great, and thanks for making supper."

"You know I like to cook and I never get much chance to do it—except at your house."

I reached for the cucumber salad and took a second helping. "Hey," I said, "if I buy blueberries, could you make some cobbler? Frank keeps talking about blueberry cobbler."

"Sure. But you probably don't need to buy any berries. I'll just mention to Scott that we want some."

"Please don't," I said. "Scott has given us so much for free that I want to visit the fruit stand and actually buy something."

"I guess that makes sense."

"Have you met his aunt and uncle?"

She nodded. "We've been there a couple of times. The uncle doesn't say much, but his aunt is real friendly and seems to get a kick out of dressing for the job."

"How, exactly?"

"You'll see when you meet her."

"Will you have time to bake this week?"

"Sure. Always have time for that."

"Just wanted to check with you first. Sometimes I don't even see you for a couple days, what with your job and—everything else in your life."

"Oh yes, my job and my friend Scott. But he hasn't been around so much lately."

"Is that a good thing or—or not?"

"It's fine with me. But he still insists that he's getting tickets for that Electric Music Festival."

"Might as well go," I said. "It could be your last chance, since you're not planning to be here next summer."

"Don't remind me," she said. "I'm missing this place already."

After work the next day I made a visit to the produce market, a place just outside of town that I had driven by numerous times but never visited. It was a pavilion, which offered shade from the sun and still caught the occasional breeze off the lake. There was much to admire. As I wandered the displays of grapes, strawberries, oranges, bananas, and even papayas, I almost forgot that I was looking for blueberries.

Then I heard a voice. "Hello, dear, can I help you find anything?" The voice came from a short, plump lady who emerged from behind a pile of watermelon. She was wearing overalls embroidered with birds and flowers, and her gray hair peeked out form beneath a straw hat trimmed with yellow daisies.

"Oh, hi," I said. "Everything looks so good that I forgot what I came for."

"Oh, that happens to people," she said. "Take your time. I'll be over by the cash register."

About ten minutes later, I was at the checkout counter. My selections were the intended blueberries, plus two pints of raspberries, and jars of honey and orange marmalade.

"Thanks so much for coming in," the woman said, smiling as she pushed the keys on an old fashioned cash register. "Are you a summer visitor?"

"No, I live right here in town," I said. "And I've been wanting to meet you. I see quite a lot of your nephew Scott—he's good friends with my stepdaughter."

"Oh, you must be Tracy Quinn—and you're talking about Brooke. She is such a lovely girl."

"She is. And aren't you lucky to have Scott here helping out."

"Yes, we are. He's with his uncle right now. They drove out to a farm to get some more sweet cherries. Those things sell out as fast as we get them. My name is Hilda, by the way."

I made small talk with Hilda until more customers demanded her attention. I told her goodbye and drove back to town, feeling contented and eating raspberries along the way.

******

As I turned onto my street, I saw a silver car parked in front of my house. Then I found Ivy Martin sprawled in a wicker chair on my porch. "Well, fancy meeting you here," she said as I mounted the porch steps.

"Shouldn't be a surprise," I said, "seeing as this is my house."

"So it is. And you are exactly the person I want to see."

"So maybe you have some hot news tip for me?"

"Maybe." Ivy got out up and opened the door for me, then followed me inside. Common courtesy demanded that I offer her a drink. Minutes later we were on the porch again, sipping iced tea and eating what was left of the raspberries.

"Tell me, Tracy, how was the wedding you attended under such duress?"

"Not as bad as I expected."

"I've got to hand it to you, girlfriend, that's one experience I've never had."

"Maybe you should put it on your bucket list."

"Guess I'll do that—attend wedding of boyfriend's ex-wife, as date of said boyfriend."

"There's one part you might especially enjoy," I said. "It's a really good reason to buy a new dress."

"And to have a makeover and then show up looking utterly fabulous. But I can't see that happening soon. Right now I don't even have a boyfriend."

"Did you break things off with Mark?"

"I did. He's in Chicago right now, so I did it all by phone—actually just left him a message telling him to go to hell."

"Has he replied?"

"Not a peep. I guess that shows he's not exactly suffering."

"Are you sure he got the message?"

"Oh yeah. Until I gave him the chop, he'd been calling me twice a day."

"Knowing you, Ivy, it won't be long until you have another man in your life."

"I'm sure you're right. But first I have to finish up some old business, and that's why I'm here. I need a telephone number—for George Antonelli."

I almost choked, wondering how I had ever gotten involved in this mess. When Ivy announced her plan to get even with Mark by seducing his father, I had hoped she was joking. But now she appeared to be dead serious. "So hand it over," she ordered. "His number."

"I don't have it – here at home."

"You must be able to get it."

"Probably I can—at the office."

"Well, good," she said. "Call me tomorrow. And don't dillydally. I need to get this show on the road."

Risking Ivy's wrath, I let the next day go by without calling her. Partly the whole business slipped my mind, but mostly I was procrastinating. I knew Frank was coming for supper, and I wanted to get his take on the situation.

Frank had said he would pick up some food, so I didn't have to think about cooking. Problem was, I never knew what he was going to bring. It all depended on where his workday had taken him. "I've got ribs and potato salad," he said when he arrived. "There's a new barbecue place in Ludington."

"Sounds good," I said, although I had been hoping for corned beef.

We took our food to the table in my back yard and I brought out a roll of paper towels in lieu of napkins. Dealing with the ribs took a lot of attention, so I decided to save the serious conversation until we got to dessert. When I brought out the blueberry cobbler, I said, "Frank, there's something I'd really like your opinion about."

"Okay," he said. "I generally have an opinion on almost everything."

"It has to do with Ivy."

"Oh no. I'm no good with advice to the lovelorn."

"She's not in any distress. But I need to give you some background first, so just bear with me, please." So while we ate dessert, I explained that George

Antonelli had tracked me down and informed me that his son Mark was married. And that he'd asked me to tell Ivy.

"I don't like to get involved in gossip," I said, "but George had a reason for wanting Ivy to know that Mark is married."

"Was it a good reason?"

"Yes, it was." I told him about the suicide of one of Mark's girlfriends.

"Oh, that's sad. So you told Ivy all of this?"

"I did."

"And how did Ivy take the news?"

"First off," I said, "she called Mark some very bad names, which I won't repeat. And now she's still upset—but she has a plan for revenge."

"If it's illegal, I don't want to know about it."

"It's not illegal, but it is devious."

"Okay," he said. "Now I'm curious."

"She plans to seduce his father."

"Well, I'll be damned."

"She doesn't have George's phone number, and she wants me to get it for her. But Frank, I don't want to get any deeper into this mess than I already am."

"I see your point."

"But I'm having trouble putting her off because, well, Ivy can be very persistent."

"Understood. I have experienced Ivy's persistence."

"So what do you think I should do?"

"This one is tricky," he said. "Let me give it some thought."

So we took our dishes inside, cleaned up the kitchen, and retired to the living room, where I steered the conversation back to the question at hand. "What do you think? Should I, or should I not, give Ivy a phone number for George Antonelli?"

"Well, here's my take on it. First of all, there's nothing illegal going on here."

"Spoken like a true officer of the law," I said. "But isn't there something a little bit, well, immoral?"

"To begin with, George Antonelli is not married."

"Right. We know he's widowed."

"And he's certainly an adult—I'd say, a competent adult."

"Right. Nowhere near senile. But is he competent enough to deal with someone like Ivy?"

"Here's what I think," said Frank. "Go head and give Ivy the number. She'll probably get it anyway."

"That's what I figured."

"But then give George a call—and tell him what's coming his way."

"What a great idea," I said. " I never thought of that."

"And then we just let the two of them work it out."

****

By the time I went to work the next day I had decided that Frank's suggestion for dealing with the Ivy/Mark/George situation was a good one. Besides, I really couldn't think of anything better. So I began with step one. Compassion dictated that I talk to George Antonelli before giving Ivy his contact information. So when I went home on my lunch hour, I called his number. (As you may have guessed, I had it all the time.) After four rings, he picked up.

"Hello, Tracy Quinn. How nice to hear from you."

"Hello yourself, George. Are you in Chicago now?"

"I am. But I'm planning to get back to Michigan in a few weeks."

"Good. That will give you time to prepare yourself."

"Prepare for what? Was the lakeshore washed away?"

"Nothing like that. It's about Ivy. As you requested, I went ahead and told her about Mark being married. And I'm pretty sure she has dumped him."

"That's good, I think."

"But here's the scary part, George. Now she has her eye on you."

"On me? Where do I fit in?"

"Here's what happened. When I told her about Mark, she thought for a little while. As I recall, she took a big swallow of her tequila and said, 'I wonder how Mark would like it if I seduced his father.'"

For a moment I thought we had lost connection. Then I heard a cough.

Finally he said, "Tracy, I'm speechless."

"And forgive me, George, but I'll be giving up your telephone number. I can't figure any way to avoid it."

"Your friend is a devious woman."

"She is. But I hope this won't keep you away from Michigan."

"That would be one way to handle things. But I like Michigan too much to stay away. Ivy doesn't know where I live, does she?"

"No, and I can't tell her because I've never been there."

"Good on that. I guess I could change my number, but that seems a bit juvenile."

"Like I said, you've got some time to figure it out. So now it's up to you."

"Okay. I'll plan my defense. Thanks for the heads up."

"I've got to cut this short because I'm on my lunch hour. But George, there's just one more thing."

"What's that?"

"We never had this conversation."

"I understand. And thanks for the call, Tracy. Now I'm beginning to think it's a little bit funny."

"Good attitude. Hang on to your sense of humor."

****

The next day was Friday, so Frank and I went out for dinner at an Italian restaurant in Wexford and he stayed overnight. In the morning, Brooke left for work so we were alone in the kitchen with our pancakes. "Hey," I said as I dug in, "Jewell was wondering if you guys ever figured out what happened out at camp—that arsenic business and all."

"Oh that," he said. "Well, it looks like we can blame the rat."

"The rat?"

"Yes, the rat. Remember we sent the baking pans to be tested?"

"I remember. What did they find?"

"They found arsenic in one of the baking pans."

"As suspected. But how did it get there? Was it the work of an unhappy camper?"

"No. The lab found arsenic in the bottom of the pan and said it was there before the food went in."

"Seems strange."

"I thought so too. But we talked with Dr. Blunt, the head of the health department, and he said there were two other cases where a rat managed to distribute arsenic before dying from it."

"Interesting. What was Dallas Bursley's response?"

"She was relieved that it wasn't any kind of sabotage. And said of course they would develop a new procedure for the kitchen—something designed to keep all the cookware and utensils better protected during the off-season."

We put our dishes to soak, poured more coffee and took our cups to the front porch. Together we surveyed the lawn and agreed that it could use the attentions of a lawnmower but could wait a few days. "How did you come out with your Ivy drama?" said Frank. "Did you give her George Antonelli's phone number?"

"I did, but I called George first to warn him."

"How did he respond?"

"He thought it was pretty funny, once he got over the shock."

"You know, there's always a chance that George might enjoy a little tumble with Ivy."

"I thought of that too. But this way he'll know exactly what's going on."

CHAPTER THIRTY-FIVE

Monday morning Frank met with Sheriff Benny in his office. It was their usual practice to kick off the week by comparing notes on outstanding cases while they drank coffee and sampled baked goods.

"Folks in town are still upset about the body on the beach," the sheriff said. "Amanda Peebles is president of the homecoming committee and she said if we don't get this resolved, it will wreck the whole weekend."

"Amanda caught up with me too," said Frank.

"I told her we were making progress," said Benny. "But are we? Have you got anything?"

"Maybe. I'm gonna talk with a guy named Jeremy—the kid who hosted that beach party."

"Good. Seems like he ought know something."

"Let's hope so. And I'm going to meet again with Zoe."

"She's the sister?" said Benny.

"Right. And the first time we talked, she told me Tony's funeral was coming up and there would be a crowd of young people. So I asked her to snoop around and see who Brandi might have been involved with before she and Tony got together."

"And you're doing this because..."

"Because there might have been a jealous ex-lover."

"Would he be mad enough to kill the new guy?"

"Stranger things have happened," said Frank. "And so far, we haven't been able to find any other good motive."

"So this sister—did she find out anything?"

"Maybe. Zoe was at the funeral, and she snooped around as I had requested. So when we met up last week she provided me with two names...of Brandi's ex- boyfriends."

"Looks like Brandi was a busy girl."

"So now I need to find them both and ask some questions."

"What are the names?"

"The names are..." Frank pulled his notebook out of his pocket. "The names are Steve Morgan and Zach Walker."

"Pretty common names," said Benny. "Anything else to help locate them?"

"Both were college students at Ferris State—at least, they were last year."

"I guess you should call the college and see if they will provide home addresses on these two."

"Believe me, I already tried," said Frank. "And they gave me a line about their policy of strict confidentiality."

"Did you say this was a murder investigation?"

"Yes, and that seemed to make things worse."

"People tend to be very skittish these days," said Benny.

******

The next morning Frank said to the sheriff, "I'm heading over to Big Rapids today. Want to come along?"

"No, but I did my best to get you through the door. I sent a registered letter to the college president and told him you would be making a visit and it was part of an important investigation."

"Thanks for that. Did you get any response?"

"I got an email," said Benny, "indicating that his office would instruct staff to cooperate with law enforcement."

"Let's hope they do," said Frank. "And then I'm going to look up this kid Jeremy, the one who hosted that beach party."

"Good. Ask him if anybody at his party wound up dead."

"That's the idea, but I'll try to be a little more subtle. What are you doing today?"

"Gotta meet with Jerry Whitmore, the state police detective."

"What's it about?"

"Haven't got a clue."

"Ha. Okay, good luck with that. I'm outta here."

"Don't get lost. Want a road map?"

"Maps are not much help in the Manistee National Forest. Last time I was heading that way I came to a sign that said *Road Closed* but offered no suggestion as to a detour."

"Like I said, good luck."

Frank made the trip to Big Rapids with few complications. He arrived at the Ferris State campus and found that most of the buildings looked much alike. He had thought he might ask someone for directions, but the place was quiet with no foot traffic. It was a little past eleven when he located the registrar's office.

Once inside, he headed for a window that said *Information*. On the other side of the glass was a young woman with short brown hair whose name tag read *TRUDY*.

Frank approached the window and said, "Hi, Trudy." He introduced himself and showed his identification. "I believe your president may have mentioned that I was coming."

"Actually, it was the vice president," she responded. "And he said I could provide you with limited information about two students."

"That's good," said Frank. "So here goes. The names are Bruce Morgan and Zach Walker." He passed her a slip of paper with the two names.

Trudy looked at the paper. "Could that one be Zachary?"

"Probably is," said Frank.

As she turned to her computer, Trudy said, "I'm authorized to give you, let's see, their date of birth, date of enrollment and a phone number, but nothing else."

"Fine. I'll take anything you can give me."

She turned to her keyboard, typed in a name and, after a few seconds said, "Okay, I found Zachary Walker. But it looks like we have two Bruce Morgans."

"Fine, I'll take them both."

"But that would make three," she said, her brow furrowed. "And I'm only authorized to give out two."

"Well, technically, it would be three," said Frank. "But I'm pretty sure it would be okay to cover two guys with the same name."

"Just a minute. I'd better ask my boss." Trudy left her post and disappeared down a hallway. Frank leaned over in an attempt to see her computer screen and found that maybe Zach Walker was having some of his credits withheld until he paid for...something.

That's when Frank noticed people behind him looking at him curiously. So he faked a big yawn and pretended to be stretching his back before he returned to a more nonchalant stance.

When Trudy returned, she said, "I've got the okay to do this for both of them." She sat down and glanced at the clock. "I have to go to lunch pretty soon."

"You must be hungry."

"Oh, I am. Didn't have any breakfast—except a cup of coffee. I'm trying to lose weight."

"I don't see why," said Frank. "You look just about right."

That won him a smile. "This will just take a minute," she said.

A printer hummed softly on the other side of the room. Trudy retrieved its offerings and handed them to Frank. He took the papers and scanned them. "Thanks a lot, Trudy," he said. "You've been a big help."

Being a college town, Big Rapids had a wide range of fast food offerings. Frank got a cheeseburger and malt at a drive-through and ate lunch as he drove to his next appointment. Within an hour he was on the outskirts of the city of Mount Pleasant. He found Jeremy Merrifield at his place of work, which turned out to be a dog-boarding facility. Jeremy was tall and lanky, wearing a faded flannel shirt and patched jeans. He had a sparse beard barely covering cheeks that showed traces of adolescent acne.

"Let's go outside," he said to Frank. "It gets noisy in here."

"Sure," said Frank. "Lead on."

Frank followed Jeremy outdoors to a shady spot with a picnic table, where their conversation was uninterrupted, except for an occasional bark or plaintive howl. "My uncle told me you were coming," Jeremy said, drumming his fingers on the table. "I hope I'm not in any trouble."

"You're not in trouble," said Frank. "But I do have some questions for you. It's about that party you had at your uncle's cottage over on the lake."

"Sure. I'll tell you everything I can."

"Okay. First of all, tell me who was there."

"Well, that's a little tricky. It certainly was a lot more people than I expected. I mean, I don't even live over there. But I had a couple of guys staying with me, and they invited some people they knew. I guess those people told their friends, and then word got around until, after a while, I couldn't even keep track of who was there. Altogether almost thirty people, maybe.

Frank pulled out his little notebook and wrote *25-30*. "Was there alcohol?"

"Sure, a lot of six packs. One bottle of Jack Daniels, and some girls brought Jell-O shots."

"Okay. Do you remember anything about—something called chex mix?"

"Oh that." Jeremy paused a moment. "Okay, here's what I remember. Somebody found a salad bowl and put it on the table, and then kids started dropping in pills and stuff. I had never heard of this business, so I didn't catch on at first. Later I saw people, mostly guys, reach in the bowl, grab some pills, and swallow them. That's when my buddy told me about something that kids are doing called chex mix. I never tried any myself."

"Okay," said Frank. "So now, down on the beach. Was there any kind of disagreement—anybody fighting?"

"I was up and down the stairs, you know, trying to get the food set up and the fire going, so there was a lot that I missed. But then, one time I came down the stairs and saw two of the guys mixing it up, they were both down in the sand; but then my friends pulled them apart and told them to cool it. And they did."

"Do you know who the guys were?"

"Sorry, I don't. It wasn't anyone I really knew, just part of the crowd that showed up."

"Did you get any idea what they were fighting about?"

Jeremy rubbed his jaw and thought for a few seconds. "All I can remember is they were cussing each other and arguing—"

"Any idea what they were arguing about?"

"I'm not sure—but it seems like they kept mentioning someone named Randy."

Frank stopped writing. "Do you think the name could have been Brandi?"

"I guess so," said Jeremy. "Well, sure, it might have been Brandi."

CHAPTER THIRTY-SIX

"Tracy, it's almost nine o'clock," Marge said when I arrived at work Thursday morning.

"Good morning to you too," I said without apology. After all, we had worked late on Wednesday to get the paper to press, so I felt that I deserved a little extra sleep.

"What are you working on today?"

"I'm writing up that feature about the Golden Oldies."

"Oh that, " she said. "That bunch of women who don't want to act their age." Personally I felt these were women to be admired. The Golden Oldies were a tap-dance troupe, all senior citizens, who got together every week for practice. "Yep," I said. "A whole dozen of them. And they perform at a lot of fund raisers."

"Yeah, sure," Marge said grudgingly. "If we don't get any bigger news this week, we'll have to put them on the front page." My editor disappeared into her office. I finished the feature story and then wrote up a piece about the newly elected president of the service club. At noon I went home for lunch, and definitely took my time, because I knew that when I got back, I would face a rather boring task.

Back at the office, I started reviewing letters to the editor. I found a sizzling complaint about the road commission, a diatribe against someone on the village council and something else so convoluted I couldn't figure what it was about. I was happy to be interrupted by Jake, our senior reporter, when he came in through the back door. "Tracy," he said, "what in blazes is going on at that farm out by Westerville?"

"I've no idea, Jake. I haven't been out there in months."

"Come on, you must know something. I saw Gus Lawford at the bakery, and he said when he drove down Warren Road he passed a whole gaggle of cars parked out there. Two of them were state cops and one was the sheriff's car, so I would surmise that Frank is out there too."

"Maybe it was a traffic accident."

"Except it wasn't. Gus said there were no lights flashing and no damaged cars. And no ambulance anywhere."

"All I know is Frank told me he was going over to Big Rapids today."

"This whole business is making me very curious," said Jake.

"What do you think is going on?" I said. "Do we have a criminal on the loose?"

"Maybe someone escaped from the county jail."

"Or maybe from that juvenile detention camp by Bitely?" This came from Marge, who had overheard us and was now joining the discussion.

"I think someone should go find out," said Jake.

"Tracy, do you want to go?" said Marge.

"Might be a job for two people," said Jake.

"Fine," said Marge, "both of you go."

"I'll drive," he said. "My camera is in the car."

Jake drove pretty fast and rolled through a couple of stop signs, but I decided not to worry since he seemed to know his way around these roads. "Jake, do you know where it is we're heading?"

"Pretty sure I do. Gus told me it was that place that used to be a pig farm. I know where that is 'cause I wrote about them one time. But nobody has lived there for years."

We traveled east on a paved road for about twenty minutes until a final turn onto gravel. The road was dry and dusty. A couple of miles in, I spotted our destination. As promised, there were half a dozen parked cars, and all of them were law enforcement. Jake parked. We got out and looked around and, as near as I could tell, all of the vehicles were empty. He grabbed his camera and was taking shots of the scene when I noticed a cloud of dust moving down the road.

At the head of the cloud of dust was a vehicle. The vehicle slowed and then came to a stop right behind Jake's car. I began to think that it looked familiar. The driver got out and walked toward us. The driver looked familiar too. My heart did a little leap when I recognized Frank Kolowsky.

"Hey there, Tracy," he said as he approached. "Hello, Jake. And what in tarnation is going on out here?"

"We're not exactly sure," I said. "We're hoping you might tell us."

****

A search was conducted Thursday of the Everham property near Westerville. Michigan State Police and the Cedar County Sheriff's Department joined forces to search for evidence concerning the disappearance of Hazel Everham. The woman was last seen in the mid 90s and the case was filed as missing-person. MSP detective Jerry Whitmore said the case was recently reopened as a homicide investigation. The search produced an item of evidence which is being analyzed. Anyone who has information about Ms. Everham is urged to call the state police at....

"Is this all we have?" Marge frowned as she read the media release.

"That's the official statement," said Jake.

"Sure, but you two went out there. Didn't you find out anything else?"

Jake shrugged. "We hung around until the sheriff came back to his car—and then Jerry Whitmore too. But nobody would talk."

"They told us to wait for the official press release," I said. "And now we have it."

"How about you, Tracy?" said Marge. "What about your inside source?"

"I talked to Frank, and he didn't know any thing," I said. "Either that or he wouldn't tell me."

"But we do have photos," said Jake.

"Well, that's something, at least," she said. "A whole phalanx of cop cars does indicate something going on. Anyway, we've got a few days to find out something more. And the weekend is coming up. So Tracy, see what you can find out from Frank."

What does she expect me to do? Get the detective drunk and pry secrets out of him?

"I'll do my best," I said.

****

Around noon Friday Ivy called and begged—no, it was more like she demanded—that I meet her for a drink after work. "I'm going to be in town," she said, "and I'm sure you can spare me an hour of your time."

Since I had no other plans, I agreed. It was a few minutes after five when I walked into the Antler Bar and found that Ivy was already there. As soon as my drink was delivered, she proposed that we move to a table outdoors.

As soon as we were seated, Ivy leaned close and said, "Tell me what you know about that business out at the pig farm."

"Honestly, Ivy, not a thing. We got the same press release today that you did."

"I thought you might have been able to get something out of Frank."

"So far, not a word." I repeated my mantra. "Either he doesn't know or he won't tell me."

Ivy regarded me with a look that said she didn't exactly believe me. "Do let me know if you find out anything."

"Of course," I said. "Don't I always share with you?"

"Moving on," she said, "how about going to the Electric Festival with me? With Mark out of the picture, I have an extra ticket—and I'd hate to let it go to waste."

"Thanks, Ivy, but I'm pretty sure it isn't anything I would enjoy. And did you ever hear back from Mark?"

"Oh, him," she said. "Since I haven't heard a peep, I guess we could say he isn't exactly heartbroken."

"Well, that's good."

"So now I'm working on his father."

"How is that coming along?" I said, though I wasn't sure I wanted to know.

"I called him, and we talked quite a long time. He won't be in back in Michigan for a couple of weeks. But when he gets here, we have a dinner date."

CHAPTER THIRTY-SEVEN

"A tooth?' said Frank. "That was their big piece of evidence?"

"That's what they found," said Benny. "It was in a feeding trough in one of the barns."

It was Monday, and Frank was in Benny's office sharing the latest news about the search at the Everham farm. "Was it a pig tooth?"

"That would hardly qualify as evidence."

"So it was what—human?"

"Sure was. First thing Jerry Whitmore did was show it to Doc Barns, the dentist, and he promised them it was human."

"So now they're thinking—what—that the tooth belonged to Hazel Everham?"

"That's what they're thinking."

"But how would her tooth end up in the hog trough?"

Benny sighed. "Frank, you're a city boy, so let me remind you of something I told you a while back. I said that pigs will eat anything."

"I remember now. But does that really mean—anything?"

Benny nodded. "Anything, including a human body."

"Oh crap," said Frank as he followed the sheriff's logic. "Are you saying that Everham killed his wife and fed her to the hogs?"

"That's what he did," said Benny, "and he nearly got away with it."

Frank shook his head. "Look at me," he said. "After thirty years on the mean streets of Detroit, I thought I had seen everything."

"So the tooth is our evidence," said Benny. "But we have to prove the tooth was hers before we can get the bastard shipped back to Michigan."

"If I remember right," said Frank, "a tooth is a good source of DNA."

"It is. And it lasts a long time."

"But now we need to match it to a relative to prove that it came from her."

"We need a female relative," said Benny. "And we've had no luck tracing the sister."

"Which looks like a problem. Didn't you say they only had one kid—the boy who died?"

"That's how I remember it," said Benny.

"So what can we do?"

"I told Jerry Whitmore that you and me might take a ride out to the Crystal Creek Tavern. Milt and Edna seem to know everything."

"Sounds good," said Frank. "Your car or mine?"

"Best we take yours," said the sheriff. "A cop car out there might discourage some of their customers." Four pickup trucks and one motorcycle were in the parking lot of the Crystal Creek Tavern when Frank and Benny arrived.

"Looks like we've hit the noon rush," said Benny.

"Let's hope they're not too busy to talk to us," said Frank.

"Not a problem," said Benny. "I called Milt and told him we were coming. He said their daughter was working today so they'd be able to take a break whenever we come by."

When Frank and Benny walked in, the owner saw them and said, "Hello, boys. Two coffees: one black, one cream, right?"

"That's right," said Benny.

As soon as the men sat down, Milt Granger brought coffee and took their orders. The food arrived shortly and, by the time Frank and the sheriff were finished eating, the place had emptied out. The only remaining customer was a guy at the bar who seemed fascinated with the lady bartender. Milt and his wife Edna, both wearing stained aprons over generous bellies, approached Frank and Benny a few minutes later. "Let's go over there," Milt said, jerking a thumb toward a back corner.

The four of them relocated to a seldom-used table. "So, what do you need to know?" Milt said as soon as they were all sitting down.

"Is this about them Everhams?" said Edna.

"You guessed right," said Benny. "I can't tell you the whole story, but it looks like Hazel may have been murdered."

"I knew it!" said Edna. She nudged her husband. "Didn't I say so?"

"Yeah, you did," said Milt. And then to the sheriff: "Was it her husband?"

"Looks that way," said Benny. "You see, we have a piece of evidence and well—maybe you've heard about DNA—"

"I sure have," said Edna.

"She likes them cop shows," said Milt.

"Okay, good," said Benny. "So what we need is to locate a blood relative of Hazel...but it needs to be a female. Seems there was a sister in Texas, but we can't find her. Do you know of any other family on her side? Can you think of anyone, or anything, that might help us?"

"Can't think of anything," Milt said as he shook his head. "She wasn't from around here."

"Oh, I can help with that," said Edna. "They had a baby daughter...but they gave her away."

"Gave her away?"

"Yep, to another couple that didn't have no kids. I don't think they ever went through the courts or anything—but it worked out okay. She's all grown up now and married."

"Does the girl know?" said Frank.

"Oh yeah, they told her when she was about ten. I think she's got the birth certificate and everything."

"This helps a lot," said Benny. "Can you help us find her?"

"Sure can," said Edna, "because she's practically family. See, she married Kenny Perkins from over by Hesperia. We was at the wedding because, well, Kenny is some kind of relation to Milt."

"He's my cousin Walter's boy."

"Right. So Kenny Perkins is a sort of a nephew to Milt."

"Can you give us her phone number?" said Benny.

"I could," said Edna, "but let me talk with her first and explain what this is all about. Otherwise you guys might just show up and scare her to death."

CHAPTER THIRTY-EIGHT

Thursday was county board meeting, which meant that I would have lunch with Ivy—unless I concocted some excuse, which I failed to do. So after the morning session, Ivy and I walked to Schooners and snagged a table. "Okay now," she said after we had ordered, "this is the day you change your mind about the festival and decide you want my extra ticket."

"Prepare to be disappointed, Ivy."

"Just yanking your chain," she said. "I sold it yesterday—to some kid who seemed pretty desperate. So I made a little profit too."

"Ivy, that makes you a scalper."

"I guess it does. But hey, I've been called worse." Conversation slowed while the waitress delivered our sandwiches. "I've got a date coming up with George Antonelli," she said. "What can you tell me about him?"

"Seems like you would know more than I do, after spending so much time with his son."

"True, but I thought maybe you could tell me a little something more."

"Here's all I can tell you: He has a cottage on Lake Michigan, but I've never been there, so don't ask me how to find it. His wife died about three years ago. He has a dog that travels with him, and he's very fond of her."

"Okay, thanks for that, and thanks for his phone number. But moving on, what do you know about that business at the pig farm?"

"Not much, I'm afraid."

"You must have heard something from Frank."

"Frank told me it is primarily a state police case but he and Benny are helping. He said there's been some progress, but he won't elaborate. Why don't you talk to Sheriff Benny?"

"I did. Brought him chocolate-chip cookies."

"What did he say?"

"He said the cookies were good. And the state police are in charge of the case—and that there have been some developments that he can't tell me about."

"So there we are. At least our sources are consistent."

"Right. And I can't get anyone at the state police to talk with me. So let me know if you find out anything."

"Don't I always, Ivy?"

****

Friday when I got home from work, I saw signs that Brooke was in the house, and wondered if she might be making supper. But cooking seemed to be the last thing on her mind. Brooke was in the living room trying to stuff some clothes into an already bulging backpack.

"Tracy," she said, "I couldn't locate a sleeping bag. I hope you don't mind if I take a couple of blankets."

"No problem, as long as you bring them back."

"Sure," she said. "I'll even wash them."

"Sounds like you're going to that music festival?"

"That's the plan. Scott has tickets, and he said they cost a bunch and he won't go unless I go with him."

"Well, that's a persuader," I said. "Did it make you feel pressured?"

"It did at first. But like you said, this'll probably be my only chance, so I might as well go. But then I had to hustle for time off. I ended up working a double shift yesterday."

"That explains why I didn't see you."

"And now I've got an early shift tomorrow. We'll leave as soon as I'm done. And do you know anyone who might lend us a tent?"

"I could talk to Jewell."

The doorbell rang. Brooke answered it and returned with a cardboard box. "I didn't feel like cooking," she said, "so I ordered a pizza. Hope that's okay with you."

"Fine with me," I said.

Before we had the box open, the telephone rang and Brooke went to answer it. She returned a minute later. "That was Scott," she said, "and the tent problem is solved. He went to Ludington and bought us a tent and air mattress."

"So you'll be camping in comfort. What a thoughtful guy."

"Yeah, pretty nice." Brooke and I sat down to eat the pizza. "But you know," she said. "There's something I keep wondering about."

"What's that?" I said, blowing on my slice to cool it down.

"Sometimes I wonder—I just wonder why Scott always seems to have money."

*****

The next afternoon a car roared into my driveway and squealed to a stop. I looked up from the book I was reading and recognized Scott's car. Brooke jumped out of the car, ran inside and grabbed her backpack. "Bye, Tracy," she said, "we're off to the Electric Festival."

"Have a great time," I said.

Frank showed up a few hours later and we headed to Manistee for a dinner event, a benefit for the fiancée of a state cop who had been killed in the line of duty. I wore my long skirt and Frank was in a sport coat. "When a cop gets killed," he said, "the survivors usually get generous benefits. But since these two weren't married, there's no provision for her. That's why we're going to this expensive dinner."

The event was at the Manistee Country Club, and I was glad we had spiffed up a bit, since everybody there was well dressed. We got drinks from the bar and then mingled while Frank introduced me to a lot of people. One of them that I already knew was Jerry Whitmore, the state police detective.

I was tempted to corner Whitmore and ask him about the pig farm business but realized that such a move would be wildly inappropriate. Eventually we took seats at a round table (nowhere near Jerry Whitmore) and enjoyed a prime-rib dinner followed by a dessert buffet with a dazzling number of choices.

CHAPTER THIRTY-EIGHT

After dinner there was an auction of donated art pieces but Frank and I left before it was over. The weather was mild and we wanted to go home by the scenic route home and stop for a walk along Lake Michigan. Also, we knew that we would have the house to ourselves when we got back to my place.

So Frank spent the night, and we probably made a little more noise than usual, knowing that Brooke was not going surprise us. In the morning we had pancakes and Frank got out the lawnmower to tend to my lawn. I pulled weeds in my garden and then we took a break, drinking lemonade on the porch as we discussed the best place to buy sweet corn.

But we never got to the sweet corn. The telephone rang and I went inside to answer. The caller didn't sound like anyone I knew so I was tempted to hang up. But I stayed on the line through a period of coughing until I realized that the caller was Brooke. Her voice was hoarse, and she sounded distraught.

"Omigod, Tracy, I'm so glad you're home. I need—I need you to come and get me. I need to get out of here."

"Aren't you at the festival?"

"Yes. I mean, no. I mean I'm at a gas station...near Roxbury. And I'm scared. Can you come and get me?"

"Sure, but can you tell me what's wrong?"

"I found out something," she said. "I'll explain when I see you. But then I'll need to talk to Frank too."

"He's right here. Shall I put him on?"

"No, no, no. Just come and get me, please. I need to get away from here."

Frank came inside about then. "We need to go and get Brooke," I said. "There's something wrong, but I don't know what. She's almost incoherent."

"Sounds like a bad trip," said Frank.

"Bad trip?"

"Sure, that whole event is built around drugs. The place is swimming with psychedelics, ecstasy, god knows what else. Everybody is stoned to the gills."

I'm sure my mouth fell open. I had thought it was just a, well, just a music festival. Recovering my voice, I said to Brooke, "Just hang on. Tell me again where you are."

"It's a Wesco gas station. Just before Roxbury."

"We'll be there."

Twenty minutes later Frank and I pulled up near a busy gas station outside Roxbury. When I climbed out of the car, I was overwhelmed by the smell of marijuana and the sound of music that was heavy on the bass. I saw a lot of scruffy looking young people but I didn't see anyone who looked like Brooke.

Finally I spotted a barefoot girl squatting against the wall between the pay phone and a pop machine. Her face was buried in her hands. "Brooke," I said, "is that you?"

She looked up and seemed to take a moment to focus. "Oh, Tracy," she said. "I'm sorry I'm such a mess." She was wearing pajama bottoms and a flannel shirt. "Can you just get me out of here?"

Frank was right beside me, so he reached down and helped her up. "Brooke, you're okay," he said in a soothing voice. "We're going to take you home."

"I'm so mixed up," she said as she looked around.

"Let's get her in the car," he said.

I put my arms around Brooke and walked her to Frank's car. He opened a rear door so we could slide in together. "How did you get here?" I said.

"I-I came with Scott, remember?"

"Sure, but how did you get here—to the phone?"

"I walked. That's why my feet are so dirty."

"Do you want to get your shoes and stuff?"

"No, no, no," she said. "I'm not going back there. Let's just go."

All the way home I kept my arms around Brooke, who was shivering, despite the eighty-degree heat. "Can you tell me what happened?" I said. "What has you so freaked out?"

She was quiet for a long time. Finally she took a deep breath. "It's about Scott," she said. "I found out something."

"Something—about Scott?"

"Yes. I think maybe he killed someone."

CHAPTER THIRTY-NINE

For the rest of the ride home, Brooke just rambled, making random references to blue butterflies and a paisley elephant. When we got to my house, we sat her at the kitchen table and Frank issued instructions. "Give her some water—or juice," he said. "She's definitely dehydrated."

I got some water from the fridge but decided it was too cold and gave her a glass of tap water instead. She made a face but drank it down and asked for more.

"When's the last time you ate anything?" he said.

"Maybe yesterday. I really can't remember."

"That means low blood sugar," he said to me. "Have you got anything sweet?"

For once we didn't have any pie or cobbler in the fridge. I found some marmalade and made a sandwich. At first Brooke looked at the food like it was a foreign object, but then she proceeded to devour it. I searched until I found some chocolate eggs left over from Easter. She ate them too. Finally her trembling stopped. "Could I take a shower," she said, "a hot shower?"

I glanced at Frank, who nodded his assent. "Sure," I said, "I'll go in with you."

So I walked with her into the bathroom, got the water started and said, "I'll run upstairs and get you some clean clothes." I went to her room, located some items, and tossed them into the bathroom. "Here you are," I said. "Need any help?"

"No, I'm good. But thanks."

Frank and I made coffee and drank it while he explained the current drug culture. "It seems you have more experience than I do with bad trips," I said. "She was fine when she left here yesterday, maybe tired—she worked extra shifts to get the time off."

"Sure, so throw in a little exhaustion too. Then last night she probably took some weird combination and has been tripping ever since. When kids get high in that setting, they tend to forget about eating or drinking."

"But does that explain why she's so upset? Why she walked away and called us?"

"No, it doesn't. And I don't think Brooke is prone to hysterics. There must be something else going on."

I went to check on Brooke and met her in the living room. She was wearing clean clothes and looked a lot more like the girl I remembered. "Hey, you look better," I said. "Do you feel better?"

"I do."

"Can you tell me what had you so freaked out?"

"Yes, but let's go in the kitchen so Frank can hear this. I only want to tell it once."

So we sat Brooke down at the kitchen table, where I gave her some herbal tea with lots of honey. "Okay, where to start. Me and Scott left here. It took forever to get into the place—had to park and carry the tent, but we finally found a spot and got set up. Tons of people, all pretty young. Would you believe there was a huge paisley elephant at the corner of our camp area? We went to one of the stages and heard a band called Plague of Locusts. Just stood and grooved cause there was no place to sit. I saw Scott talking to a guy who gave him something, but I didn't pay much attention. When Scott handed me a brownie, I ate it. I figured there was weed in it but, what the heck, we were there for the night. Someone else passed around a pipe and I had a hit from that too.

"We walked to another stage that had a backdrop of huge flowers and guitars and stuff. Pretty soon the colors started smooshing into each other. Everywhere we went there was more trippy stuff going on—a place called Sherwood Forest, with hammocks hanging from the trees. We scored one of the hammocks and just hung out for a while. A drum circle started and that made me want to dance...so I did.

"No idea what time it was, but eventually the sun went down and things got real spooky. There were fairy lights in all the trees, and I think we saw some fire dancers. Once in a while I'd lose Scott and then we'd find each other. No idea when we finally headed back to our tent. We got lost a few times but finally found our way back to the elephant. Then we crashed.

"No idea when we woke up, but it was daylight. Scott brought me something to drink. It tasted kind of nasty, but he said it had plenty of caffeine. There was already a band playing, so we went out and saw some belly dancers and acrobats. Before too long, I said I needed to crash. So we walked back to the tent and went to sleep.

"When I woke up it was hot in the tent, I was sweating, and Scott was gone. I found that I was sleeping with a pair of his jeans under my head. I sort of remembered him changing clothes...putting on some shorts. But then, you know, I wasn't really snooping, but his wallet was lying right on the floor of the tent and he had so many cards that a lot of them had slipped out. I figured I would put them back —and that's when I noticed that he had someone else's driver's license. The license was for Anthony Braxton. Wasn't that the guy who drowned?"

"Yes it was," said Frank. "Tony Braxton."

"So I started thinking—if Scott had the guy's ID and stuff, then maybe Scott was the one who killed him—and then I thought—if Scott knew that I knew, he might try to hurt me too."

"Sure," said Frank, "your mind was racing." To me he said, "Paranoia is common."

"What's more," said Brooke, "I saw his real drivers license and found out that Scott's first name is Zachary. He's been going by his middle name."

"Zachary?" said Frank. "Are you sure?"

"The license said Zachary Scott Walker."

"Zach Walker," he repeated. "Brooke, my girl, I think you have just cracked our case."

CHAPTER FORTY

"The guy has been right under our nose the whole time," said Frank. He stood abruptly. "I need to call the sheriff. Where did I leave my cell phone?"

"I think it's in my bedroom," I said, recalling our late-night romp. "Maybe on the floor."

Minutes later I heard him talking to Sheriff Benny. "Shouldn't be hard to pick him up," he said. "He's at that music festival, and there are only two exits. And you know, we've got law enforcement all over the place.

"Right. His name is Zachary Walker. But he may show an ID for Anthony Braxton. And he'll be driving...hey, Brooke, tell me about his car. It's a Ford sedan...four-door, gray, pretty old—she doesn't know the year."

Minutes later Frank was on his way out the door. "Take care of Brooke," he said. "More fluids to flush out her system and then she'll want to sleep a lot. And remind her that she's done a good thing."

****

I called in to work on Monday and said I was taking the day off due to a family emergency. It sounded good, though almost everyone knew I had no family in the area—come to think of it, no family anywhere. But Brooke was definitely family. And I was not about to leave her alone.

For the second time that summer, she ended up sleeping in my bed. She slept like the proverbial log, so the arrangement did not keep me awake. When Brooke finally rolled out, she found me in the kitchen. She poured herself a cup of coffee and said, "What happened? Did Scott—did they arrest him?"

"I haven't heard anything yet," I said. "I really want to call Frank, but I'm trying to just let him do his job. If I don't hear by noon, I'll make the call."

Shortly afterward, my phone rang. "Frank," I said, "what happened—did you find Scott?"

"Yes, we did, and he's now lodged at the Cedar County Jail. How is Brooke doing?"

"Mostly recovered—as far as the physical part. But still in a lot of emotional turmoil. Can you come by sometime and talk to her?"

"Sure, I'll come right after work."

When Brooke heard that Frank was coming, she wanted to make macaroni and cheese for supper. I agreed because she seemed to need a project. Also, I felt we could all benefit from a meal of solid comfort food. The cooking kept Brooke busy most of the afternoon but was finished by the time Frank arrived. And that was good, because when they started to talk, she broke down crying.

"I just feel so guilty," she said. "And then I feel creeped out all over again—I mean, I spent all that time with him—my lord, we slept together for a month. How could I have been so blind?"

"Don't feel bad," said Frank. "He had everybody fooled. Even me."

"And me," I said. "I thought he was such a charming young man."

"It's still hard for me to believe that he could kill somebody," she said. "What will happen to him?"

"Depends on his lawyer," said Frank, "and the judge. There's a good chance the charges will be reduced to manslaughter. Benny said that Scott keeps claiming it was just an accident. That he and his friend went swimming and Tony just never came out."

"But he never told anyone on the beach that his friend was in trouble," I said.

"And he helped himself to the guy's cash, ID, and credit cards," said Frank.

"What about Tony's clothes?" I said. "Do you think Scott deliberately hid them?"

"Looks that way," said Frank. "They were a long way from the bonfire. So he's got a lot to answer for. I'd say it was not premeditated, but he certainly took advantage of the circumstances."

"There's something I'm wondering," I said. "Remember, Tony's picture was in the paper and we showed it to Derek. He said he didn't see him at the party."

"I remember," said Frank. "But how many kids still look like their high school photo a few years later? Not many."

"You're right. Most of them are eager to lose that wholesome image."

"So, Brooke," he said, "we owe you a great big thanks for solving this case."

"I'm glad I could help," she said with a sigh. "But sometimes, I just feel guilty."

"You feel guilty for—outing a killer?"

"Yes. I mean, no. I guess I don't know how I should feel."

Brooke was close to tears again. "I know what we all need," I said.

"What's that?"

"We need some hot, gooey macaroni and cheese—and I think Frank brought some chocolate fudge ice cream."

"Sounds good," said Brooke. "And then I want to call Derek."

CHAPTER FORTY-ONE

"Grampa, Grampa, tell us a story."

"Tell us a ghost story."

"No, tell us a real story."

The hot dogs had been devoured, the marshmallows set on fire and smashed into s'mores. The sun had slipped away, so Frank and I were sitting with Pete and Luke around a campfire on the promised overnight.

"Tell us a real story, about catching some bad guys."

"Shall I tell them about the hog farm?" he whispered to me.

"No, that's too creepy."

"Okay. I'll tell you a story about one time when I tried to rescue Tracy—from the hands of a killer, of course—and for thanks, she tried to break my nose."

"Did you really break his nose, Tracy?"

"It was an accident," I said.

"She claims she didn't know it was me."

"So she thought you were the bad guy?"

"Yep. Though in this case, a woman was the bad guy."

"Oh, tell us about that."

"Okay, here we go. It all started one evening when I had a date with Tracy. I showed up at her house, and she wasn't home. So I went inside, got comfortable, and waited."

"I think he found a beer in the fridge," I added.

"Well, maybe. Anyway, it was getting late, and I hadn't heard from her, so I did a bit of detective work; I played the messages on her answering machine. The last message was from her friend Jewell. Jewell said she was going to meet someone at the village museum.

"I decided to drive over to the museum and check things out. The place is normally empty at night, but there were lights on and two cars parked outside. One of them was Tracy's. So I parked and walked inside.

"Now, inside the building there was a little hallway, and at the end of that was another door. When I opened the second door and tried to walk through, someone hit me in the face and threw a bag over my head."

"I didn't hit him hard," I explained. "It was all an accident, because he was not the person I was expecting."

"When I got the thing off my head, I saw it was Tracy. I didn't understand what was going on, but Jewell was there too, and they showed me bullet holes in the wall. So I started to believe the ladies when they said that a woman had lured Jewell there and tried to kill her. And that woman had just left the building."

"Did she get away?"

"Well, boys, we all got in my car and went racing off to try and catch up with her. But it was winter, you see, and the roads were icy, and what happened was that her car went off that bridge just outside of town. When we arrived at the bridge, her car was in the water. There was already a cop car there, and an ambulance and a wrecker, and our good friend Derek was pulling her out of the water. And she went to jail. End of story."

"Tell us another one."

"Not tonight. It's time for you boys to crawl into your sleeping bags. But go pee in the woods first."

"Really?"

"Sure. If you were home you would do that before bed, wouldn't you?"

"Yes, and brush our teeth too."

"You can forget about that part."

"What if we get scared?"

"There's nothing to be scared of, and besides, Tracy and I are right here, just a few feet away."

After the boys were zipped into their tent and sleeping bags, Frank and I watched the fire die down and then made certain it was out. "Did Ivy ever have her date with George Antonelli?" said Frank.

I laughed. "Ivy told me they went out to dinner and he was a perfect gentleman. She tried to lure him into her place for a drink, but he declined."

"Ivy's not accustomed to being refused."

"Right," I said. "This could be an interesting saga."

Frank and I crawled into our own tent and settled into a deluxe accommodation called a double sleeping bag. "About the pig farm," I said. "Did they catch that guy— the one who fed his wife to the hogs?"

"*Allegedly* fed his wife to the hogs. And yes, he's in jail in Oregon. Trying not to get extradited to Michigan—but it's just a matter of time."

"I hope I get to cover that trial," I said and then yawned. "It's been a long day."

"Yes, it has. And thanks for putting up with those two."

That's when we heard a small voice from the other tent. "Grampa?"

"Just ignore them," Frank whispered.

And another voice, even smaller. "Grampa?"

"What??"

"Are you and Tracy gonna get married?"

"You boys just go to sleep," he said with a groan.

"I think they're fixated on weddings," I whispered.

I was almost asleep when Frank nuzzled my ear and said, "So how about it?"

"How about—what?"

"Are we gonna get married?"

"Frank, just go to sleep."

About the Author

Sally DeFreitas grew up on a farm in West Michigan, became a nurse, and worked in San Francisco and Miami Beach before succumbing to the call of the sea. She explored Caribbean islands and Mediterranean ports while working on vessels that ranged from private yachts to a tugboat. On her return to Michigan, she again worked as a nurse, then spent ten years as a journalist before retiring to write books and play guitar.This is the fifth installment in her Tracy Quinn mystery series.

You can connect with me on:

https://www.facebook.com/sally.defreitas

Made in the USA
Columbia, SC
09 August 2021